An Outpost of Progress
and Other Stories

AN OUTPOST OF PROGRESS
AND OTHER STORIES

DOVER THRIFT EDITIONS

Joseph Conrad

DOVER PUBLICATIONS, INC.
MINEOLA, NEW YORK

DOVER THRIFT EDITIONS

GENERAL EDITOR: SUSAN L. RATTINER
EDITOR OF THIS VOLUME: STEPHANIE CASTILLO SAMOY

Copyright

Bibliographical Note

An Outpost of Progress and Other Stories is a new compilation of works by Joseph Conrad, reprinted from authoritative sources.

Library of Congress Cataloging-in-Publication Data

Names: Conrad, Joseph, 1857–1924, author.
Title: An outpost of progress and other stories / Joseph Conrad.
Description: Mineola, New York : Dover Publications, [2019] |
Series: Dover thrift editions
Identifiers: LCCN 2018057906 | ISBN 9780486831695 (paperback) |
ISBN 0486831698 (paperback)
Subjects: | BISAC: FICTION / Classics.
Classification: LCC PR6005.O4 A6 2019 | DDC 823/.912—dc23
LC record available at https://lccn.loc.gov/2018057906

Manufactured in the United States by LSC Communications
83169801 2019
www.doverpublications.com

Note

JOSEPH CONRAD is considered one of the greatest English-language novelists, though English was his third language (Polish and French were his first and second).

He was born Józef Teodor Konrad Korzeniowski, near Berdichev in the Polish Ukraine in 1857, during the Russian occupation. He was orphaned at the age of eleven and eventually joined the British merchant service, becoming a master mariner and a naturalized British subject by 1886. By the time his first novel was accepted for publication in 1894, Conrad had spent nearly twenty years as a sailor, and his life at sea and his experience in foreign ports furnished the background for his writing.

His fiction, which for the most part depicts the life of the seaman in the second half of the nineteenth century, takes as its preeminent themes human isolation and solidarity, the relationship between established moral codes and personal needs and desires, and the sometimes enlightening, sometimes devastating effects of extreme physical and psychological stress. Conrad also shows a deep and troubled awareness of the nature of colonialism, in particular the questions raised about Western values and self-understanding by contact with African and Asian cultures.

The stories included in this exclusive volume all draw heavily on Conrad's own experiences and are generally considered among his finest achievements in the genre.

Conrad died in 1924 at the age of sixty-six. Inscribed on his gravestone are lines from Edmund Spenser's epic poem "The Faerie Queene":

Sleep after toyle, port after stormie seas,
Ease after warre, death after life, doth greatly please.

Contents

An Outpost of Progress
and Other Stories

AN OUTPOST OF PROGRESS

1

THERE WERE TWO white men in charge of the trading station.

Kayerts, the chief, was short and fat; Carlier, the assistant, was tall, with a large head and a very broad trunk perched upon a long pair of thin legs. The third man on the staff was a Sierra Leone nigger, who maintained that his name was Henry Price. However, for some reason or other, the natives down the river had given him the name of Makola, and it stuck to him through all his wanderings about the country. He spoke English and French with a warbling accent, wrote a beautiful hand, understood bookkeeping, and cherished in his innermost heart the worship of evil spirits. His wife was a negress from Loanda, very large and very noisy. Three children rolled about in sunshine before the door of his low, shedlike dwelling. Makola, taciturn and impenetrable, despised the two white men. He had charge of a small clay storehouse with a dried-grass roof, and pretended to keep a correct account of beads, cotton cloth, red kerchiefs, brass wire, and other trade goods it contained. Besides the storehouse and Makola's hut, there was only one large building in the cleared ground of the station. It was built neatly of reeds, with a veranda on all the four sides. There were three rooms in it. The one in the middle was the living room, and had two rough tables and a few stools in it. The other two were the bedrooms for the white men. Each had a bedstead and a mosquito net for all furniture. The plank floor was littered with the belongings of the white men; open half-empty boxes, torn wearing apparel, old boots; all the things dirty, and all the things broken, that accumulate mysteriously round untidy men.

There was also another dwelling-place some distance away from the buildings. In it, under a tall cross much out of the perpendicular, slept the man who had seen the beginning of all this; who had planned and had watched the construction of this outpost of progress.

He had been, at home, an unsuccessful painter who, weary of pursuing fame on an empty stomach, had gone out there through high protections. He had been the first chief of that station.

Makola had watched the energetic artist die of fever in the just finished house with his usual kind of "I told you so" indifference.

Then, for a time, he dwelt alone with his family, his account books, and the Evil Spirit that rules the lands under the equator.

He got on very well with his god. Perhaps he had propitiated him by a promise of more white men to play with, by and by. At any rate the director of the Great Trading Company, coming up in a steamer that resembled an enormous sardine box with a flat-roofed shed erected on it, found the station in good order, and Makola as usual quietly diligent. The director had the cross put up over the first agent's grave, and appointed Kayerts to the post. Carlier was told off as second in charge. The director was a man ruthless and efficient, who at times, but very imperceptibly, indulged in grim humor. He made a speech to Kayerts and Carlier, pointing out to them the promising aspect of their station. The nearest trading post was about three hundred miles away. It was an exceptional opportunity for them to distinguish themselves and to earn percentages on the trade. This appointment was a favor done to beginners. Kayerts was moved almost to tears by his director's kindness. He would, he said, by doing his best, try to justify the flattering confidence, etcetera, etcetera. Kayerts had been in the Administration of the Telegraphs, and knew how to express himself correctly. Carlier, an ex-non-commissioned officer of cavalry in an army guaranteed from harm by several European Powers, was less impressed. If there were commissions to get, so much the better; and, trailing a sulky glance over the river, the forests, the impenetrable bush that seemed to cut off the station from the rest of the world, he muttered between his teeth, "We shall see, very soon."

Next day, some bales of cotton goods and a few cases of provisions having been thrown on shore, the sardine-box steamer went off, not to return for another six months. On the deck the director touched his cap to the two agents, who stood on the bank waving their hats, and turning to an old servant of the Company on his passage to headquarters, said, "Look at those two imbeciles. They must be mad at home to send me such specimens. I told those fellows to plant a vegetable garden, build new storehouses and fences, and construct a landing-stage. I bet nothing will be done! They won't know how to begin. I always thought the station on this river useless, and they just fit the station!" "

They will form themselves there," said the old stager with a quiet smile.

"At any rate, I am rid of them for six months," retorted the director.

The two men watched the steamer round the bend, then, ascending arm in arm the slope of the bank, returned to the station.

They had been in this vast and dark country only a very short time, and as yet always in the midst of other white men, under the eye and guidance of their superiors. And now, dull as they were to the subtle influences of surroundings, they felt themselves very much alone, when suddenly left unassisted to face the wilderness; a wilderness rendered more strange, more incomprehensible by the mysterious glimpses of the vigorous life it contained. They were two perfectly insignificant and incapable individuals, whose existence is only rendered possible through the high organization of civilized crowds. Few men realize that their life, the very essence of their character, their capabilities and their audacities, are only the expression of their belief in the safety of their surroundings. The courage, the composure, the confidence; the emotions and principles; every great and every insignificant thought belongs not to the individual but to the crowd: to the crowd that believes blindly in the irresistible force of its institutions and of its morals, in the power of its police and of its opinion. But the contact with pure unmitigated savagery, with primitive nature and primitive man, brings sudden and profound trouble into the heart. To the sentiment of being alone of one's kind, to the clear perception of the loneliness of one's thoughts, of one's sensations—to the negation of the habitual, which is safe, there is added the affirmation of the unusual, which is dangerous; a suggestion of things vague, uncontrollable, and repulsive, whose discomposing intrusion excites the imagination and tries the civilized nerves of the foolish and the wise alike.

Kayerts and Carlier walked arm in arm, drawing close to one another as children do in the dark; and they had the same, not altogether unpleasant, sense of danger which one half suspects to be imaginary. They chatted persistently in familiar tones. "Our station is prettily situated," said one. The other assented with enthusiasm, enlarging volubly on the beauties of the situation. Then they passed near the grave. "Poor devil!" said Kayerts. "He died of fever, didn't he?" muttered Carlier, stopping short. "Why," retorted Kayerts, with indignation, "I've been told that the fellow exposed himself recklessly to the sun. The climate here, everybody says, is not at all worse than at home, as long as you keep out of the sun. Do you hear that, Carlier? I am chief here, and my orders are that you should not expose yourself to the sun!" He assumed his superiority jocularly, but his meaning was serious. The idea that he would, perhaps, have to bury Carlier and remain alone, gave him an inward shiver. He felt suddenly that this Carlier was more precious to him here, in the center of Africa, than a brother could be anywhere else.

Carlier, entering into the spirit of the thing, made a military salute and answered in a brisk tone, "Your orders shall be attended to, chief!" Then he burst out laughing, slapped Kayerts on the back and shouted, "We shall let life run easily here! Just sit still and gather in the ivory those savages will bring. This country has its good points, after all!" They both laughed loudly while Carlier thought: "That poor Kayerts; he is so fat and unhealthy. It would be awful if I had to bury him here. He is a man I respect." . . . Before they reached the veranda of their house they called one another "my dear fellow." The first day they were very active, pottering about with hammers and nails and red calico, to put up curtains, make their house habitable and pretty; resolved to settle down comfortably to their new life. For them an impossible task. To grapple effectually with even purely material problems requires more serenity of mind and more lofty courage than people generally imagine. No two beings could have been more unfitted for such a struggle. Society, not from any tenderness, but because of its strange needs, had taken care of those two men, forbidding them all independent thought, all initiative, all departure from routine; and forbidding it under pain of death. They could only live on condition of being machines.

And now, released from the fostering care of men with pens behind the ears, or of men with gold lace on the sleeves, they were like those lifelong prisoners who, liberated after many years, do not know what use to make of their freedom. They did not know what use to make of their faculties, being both, through want of practice, incapable of independent thought.

At the end of two months Kayerts often would say, "If it was not for my Melie, you wouldn't catch me here." Melie was his daughter. He had thrown up his post in the Administration of the Telegraphs, though he had been for seventeen years perfectly happy there, to earn a dowry for his girl. His wife was dead, and the child was being brought up by his sisters. He regretted the streets, the pavements, the cafés, his friends of many years; all the things he used to see, day after day; all the thoughts suggested by familiar things—the thoughts effortless, monotonous, and soothing of a Government clerk; he regretted all the gossip, the small enmities, the mild venom, and the little jokes of Government offices.

"If I had had a decent brother-in-law," Carlier would remark, "a fellow with a heart, I would not be here." He had left the army and had made himself so obnoxious to his family by his laziness and impudence, that an exasperated brother-in-law had made superhuman efforts to procure him an appointment in the Company as a second-class agent. Having not a penny in the world he was compelled to accept this means of livelihood as soon as it became quite clear to him that there was nothing more to squeeze out of his relations. He, like Kayerts, regretted his old life. He regretted the clink of saber and spurs on a fine afternoon, the barrack-room witticisms, the girls of garrison towns; but, besides, he had also a sense of grievance. He was evidently a much ill-used man. This made him moody, at times. But the two men got on well together in the fellowship of their stupidity and laziness. Together they did nothing, absolutely nothing, and enjoyed the sense of the idleness for which they were paid. And in time they came to feel something resembling affection for one another.

They lived like blind men in a large room, aware only of what came in contact with them (and of that only imperfectly), but unable to see the general aspect of things. The river, the forest, all the great land throbbing with life, were like a great emptiness.

Even the brilliant sunshine disclosed nothing intelligible. Things appeared and disappeared before their eyes in an unconnected and aimless kind of way. The river seemed to come from nowhere and flow nowhither. It flowed through a void. Out of that void, at times, came canoes, and men with spears in their hands would suddenly crowd the yard of the station. They were naked, glossy black, ornamented with snowy shells and glistening brass wire, perfect of limb. They made an uncouth babbling noise when they spoke, moved in a stately manner, and sent quick, wild glances out of their startled, never-resting eyes. Those warriors would squat in long rows, four or more deep, before the veranda, while their chiefs bargained for hours with Makola over an elephant tusk.

Kayerts sat on his chair and looked down on the proceedings, understanding nothing. He stared at them with his round blue eyes, called out to Carlier, "Here, look! look at that fellow there—and that other one, to the left. Did you ever such a face? Oh, the funny brute!" Carlier, smoking native tobacco in a short wooden pipe, would swagger up twirling his mustaches, and surveying the warriors with haughty indulgence, would say—

"Fine animals. Brought any bone? Yes? It's not any too soon. Look at the muscles of that fellow third from the end. I wouldn't care to get a punch on the nose from him. Fine arms, but legs no good below the knee. Couldn't make cavalry men of them." And after glancing down complacently at his own shanks, he always concluded: "Pah! Don't they stink! You, Makola! Take that herd over to the fetish" (the store-house was in every station called the fetish, perhaps because of the spirit of civilization it contained) "and give them up some of the rubbish you keep there. I'd rather see it full of bone than full of rags."

Kayerts approved.

"Yes, yes! Go and finish that palaver over there, Mr. Makola. I will come round when you are ready, to weigh the tusk. We must be careful." Then turning to his companion: "This is the tribe that lives down the river; they are rather aromatic. I remember, they had been once before here. D'ye hear that row? What a fellow has got to put up with in this dog of a country! My head is split."

Such profitable visits were rare. For days the two pioneers of trade and progress would look on their empty courtyard in the vibrating brilliance of vertical sunshine. Below the high bank, the silent river flowed on glittering and steady. On the sands in the middle of the stream, hippos and alligators sunned themselves side by side. And stretching away in all directions, surrounding the insignificant cleared spot of the trading post, immense forests, hiding fateful complications of fantastic life, lay in the eloquent silence of mute greatness. The two men understood nothing, cared for nothing but for the passage of days that separated them from the steamer's return. Their predecessor had left some torn books. They took up these wrecks of novels, and, as they had never read anything of the kind before, they were surprised and amused. Then during long days there were interminable and silly discussions about plots and personages. In the center of Africa they made acquaintance of Richelieu and of d'Artagnan, of Hawk's Eye and of Father Goriot, and of many other people. All these imaginary personages became subjects for gossip as if they had been living friends. They discounted their virtues, suspected their motives, decried their successes; were scandalized at their duplicity or were doubtful about their courage. The accounts of crimes filled them with indignation, while tender or pathetic passages moved them deeply. Carlier cleared his throat and said in a soldierly voice, "What nonsense!" Kayerts, his round eyes suffused with tears, his fat cheeks quivering, rubbed his bald head, and declared. "This is a splendid book. I had no idea there were such clever fellows in the world." They also found some old copies of a home paper.

That print discussed what it was pleased to call "Our Colonial Expansion" in high-flown language. It spoke much of the rights and duties of civilization, of the sacredness of the civilizing work, and extolled the merits of those who went about bringing light, and faith and commerce to the dark places of the earth. Carlier and Kayerts read, wondered, and began to think better of themselves.

Carlier said one evening, waving his hand about, "In a hundred years, there will be perhaps a town here. Quays, and warehouses, and barracks, and—and—billiard rooms. Civilization, my boy, and virtue—and all. And then, chaps will read that two good fellows, Kayerts and Carlier, were the first civilized men to live in this very spot!" Kayerts nodded, "Yes, it is a consolation to think of that." They seemed to forget their dead predecessor; but, early one day, Carlier went out and replanted the cross firmly. "It used to make me squint whenever I walked that way," he explained to Kayerts over the morning coffee. "It made me squint, leaning over so much. So I just planted it upright. And solid, I promise you! I suspended myself with both hands to the cross-piece. Not a move. Oh, I did that properly."

At times Gobila came to see them. Gobila was the chief of the neighboring villages. He was a gray-headed savage, thin and black, with a white cloth round his loins and a mangy panther skin hanging over his back. He came up with long strides of his skeleton legs, swinging a staff as tall as himself, and, entering the common room of the station, would squat on his heels to the left of the door. There he sat, watching Kayerts, and now and then making a speech which the other did not understand. Kayerts, without interrupting his occupation, would from time to time say in a friendly manner: "How goes it, you old image?" and they would smile at one another.

The two whites had a liking for that old and incomprehensible creature, and called him Father Gobila. Gobila's manner was paternal, and he seemed really to love all white men. They all appeared to him very young, indistinguishably alike (except for stature), and he knew that they were all brothers, and also immortal. The death of the artist, who was the first white man whom he knew intimately, did not disturb this belief, because he was firmly convinced that the white stranger had pretended to die and got himself buried for some mysterious purpose of his own, into which it was useless to inquire.

Perhaps it was his way of going home to his own country? At any rate, these were his brothers, and he transferred his absurd affection to them. They returned it in a way. Carlier slapped him on the back, and recklessly struck off matches for his amusement. Kayerts was always ready to let him have a sniff at the ammonia bottle. In short, they behaved just like that other white creature that had hidden itself in a hole in the ground. Gobila considered them attentively. Perhaps they were the same being with the other—or one of them was. He couldn't decide—clear up that mystery; but he remained always very friendly. In consequence of that friendship the women of Gobila's village walked in single file through the reedy grass, bringing every morning to the station, fowls, and sweet potatoes, and palm wine, and sometimes a goat. The Company never provisions the stations fully, and the agents required those local supplies to live.

They had them through the goodwill of Gobila, and lived well.

Now and then one of them had a bout of fever, and the other nursed him with gentle devotion. They did not think much of it. It left them weaker, and their appearance changed for the worse.

Carlier was hollow-eyed and irritable. Kayerts showed a drawn, flabby face above the rotundity of his stomach, which gave him a weird aspect. But being constantly together, they did not notice the change that took place gradually in their appearance, and also in their dispositions.

Five months passed in that way.

Then, one morning, as Kayerts and Carlier, lounging in their chairs under the veranda, talked about the approaching visit of the steamer, a knot of armed men came out of the forest and advanced toward the station. They were strangers to that part of the country. They were tall, slight, draped classically from neck to heel in blue fringed cloths, and carried percussion muskets over their bare right shoulders. Makola showed signs of excitement, and ran out of the storehouse (where he spent all his days) to meet these visitors. They came into the courtyard and looked about them with steady, scornful glances. Their leader, a powerful and determined-looking negro with bloodshot eyes, stood in front of the veranda and made a long speech. He gesticulated much, and ceased very suddenly.

There was something in his intonation, in the sounds of the long sentences he used, that startled the two whites. It was like a reminiscence of something not exactly familiar, and yet resembling the speech of civilized men. It sounded like one of those impossible languages which sometimes we hear in our dreams.

"What lingo is that?" said the amazed Carlier. "In the first moment I fancied the fellow was going to speak French. Anyway, it is a different kind of gibberish to what we ever heard."

"Yes," replied Kayerts. "Hey, Makola, what does he say? Where do they come from? Who are they?"

But Makola, who seemed to be standing on hot bricks, answered hurriedly, "I don't know. They come from very far. Perhaps Mrs. Price will understand. They are perhaps bad men."

The leader, after waiting for a while, said something sharply to Makola, who shook his head. Then the man, after looking round, noticed Makola's hut and walked over there. The next moment Mrs. Makola was heard speaking with great volubility. The other strangers—they were six in all—strolled about with an air of ease, put their heads through the door of the storeroom, congregated round the grave, pointed understandingly at the cross, and generally made themselves at home.

"I don't like those chaps—and, I say, Kayerts, they must be from the coast; they've got firearms," observed the sagacious Carlier.

Kayerts also did not like those chaps. They both, for the first time, became aware that they lived in conditions where the unusual may be dangerous, and that there was no power on earth outside of themselves to stand between them and the unusual.

They became uneasy, went in and loaded their revolvers. Kayerts said, "We must order Makola to tell them to go away before dark."

The strangers left in the afternoon, after eating a meal prepared for them by Mrs. Makola. The immense woman was excited, and talked much with the visitors. She rattled away shrilly, pointing here and there at the forests and at the river. Makola sat apart and watched. At times he got up and whispered to his wife. He accompanied the strangers across the ravine at the back of the station-ground, and returned slowly looking very thoughtful. When questioned by the white men he was very strange, seemed not to understand, seemed to have forgotten French—seemed to have forgotten how to speak altogether. Kayerts and Carlier agreed that the nigger had had too much palm wine.

There was some talk about keeping a watch in turn, but in the evening everything seemed so quiet and peaceful that they retired as usual. All night they were disturbed by a lot of drumming in the villages. A deep, rapid roll near by would be followed by another far off—then all ceased. Soon short appeals would rattle out here and there, then all mingle together, increase, become vigorous and sustained, would spread out over the forest, roll through the night, unbroken and ceaseless, near and far, as if the whole land had been one immense drum booming out steadily an appeal to heaven.

And through the deep and tremendous noise sudden yells that resembled snatches of songs from a madhouse darted shrill and high in discordant jets of sound which seemed to rush far above the earth and drive all peace from under the stars.

Carlier and Kayerts slept badly. They both thought they had heard shots fired during the night—but they could not agree as to the direction. In the morning Makola was gone somewhere. He returned about noon with one of yesterday's strangers, and eluded all Kayerts' attempts to close with him: had become deaf apparently.

Kayerts wondered. Carlier, who had been fishing off the bank, came back and remarked while he showed his catch, "The niggers seem to be in a deuce of a stir; I wonder what's up. I saw about fifteen canoes cross the river during the two hours I was there fishing." Kayerts, worried, said, "Isn't this Makola very queer today?" Carlier advised, "Keep all our men together in case of some trouble."

2

THERE WERE TEN station men who had been left by the Director.

Those fellows, having engaged themselves to the Company for six months (without having any idea of a month in particular and only a very faint notion of time in general), had been serving the cause of progress for upwards of two years. Belonging to a tribe from a very distant part of the land of darkness and sorrow, they did not run away, naturally supposing that as wandering strangers they would be killed by the inhabitants of the country; in which they were right. They lived in straw huts on the slope of a ravine overgrown with reedy grass, just behind the station buildings. They were not happy, regretting the festive incantations, the sorceries, the human sacrifices of their own land; where they also had parents, brothers, sisters, admired chiefs, respected magicians, loved friends, and other ties supposed generally to be human. Besides, the rice rations served out by the Company did not agree with them, being a food unknown to their land, and to which they could not get used. Consequently they were unhealthy and miserable.

Had they been of any other tribe they would have made up their minds to die—for nothing is easier to certain savages than suicide—and so have escaped from the puzzling difficulties of existence.

But belonging, as they did, to a warlike tribe with filed teeth, they had more grit, and went on stupidly living through disease and sorrow. They did very little work, and had lost their splendid physique. Carlier and Kayerts doctored them assiduously without being able to bring them back into condition again. They were mustered every morning and told off to different tasks—grass-cutting, fence-building, tree-felling, etcetera, etcetera, which no power on earth could induce them to execute efficiently. The two whites had practically very little control over them.

In the afternoon Makola came over to the big house and found Kayerts watching three heavy columns of smoke rising above the forests. "What is that?" asked Kayerts. "Some villages burn," answered Makola, who seemed to have regained his wits. Then he said abruptly: "We have got very little ivory; bad six months' trading. Do you like get a little more ivory?"

"Yes," said Kayerts, eagerly. He thought of percentages which were low.

"Those men who came yesterday are traders from Loanda who have got more ivory than they can carry home. Shall I buy? I know their camp."

"Certainly," said Kayerts. "What are those traders?"

"Bad fellows," said Makola, indifferently. "They fight with people, and catch women and children. They are bad men, and got guns. There is a great disturbance in the country. Do you want ivory?"

"Yes," said Kayerts. Makola said nothing for a while. Then: "Those workmen of ours are no good at all," he muttered, looking round. "Station in very bad order, sir. Director will growl. Better get a fine lot of ivory, then he say nothing."

"I can't help it; the men won't work," said Kayerts. "When will you get that ivory?"

"Very soon," said Makola. "Perhaps tonight. You leave it to me, and keep indoors, sir. I think you had better give some palm wine to our men to make a dance this evening. Enjoy themselves. Work better tomorrow. There's plenty palm wine—gone a little sour."

Kayerts said "yes," and Makola, with his own hands carried big calabashes to the door of his hut. They stood there till the evening, and Mrs. Makola looked into every one. The men got them at sunset. When Kayerts and Carlier retired, a big bonfire was flaring before the men's huts. They could hear their shouts and drumming.

Some men from Gobila's village had joined the station hands, and the entertainment was a great success.

Only one. Carlier ran out and met Kayerts on the veranda.

They were both startled. As they went across the yard to call Makola, they saw shadows moving in the night. One of them cried, "Don't shoot! It's me, Price." Then Makola appeared close to them. "Go back, go back, please," he urged, "you spoil all." "There are strange men about," said Carlier. "Never mind; I know," said Makola. Then he whispered, "All right. Bring ivory. Say nothing! I know my business." The two white men reluctantly went back to the house, but did not sleep. They heard footsteps, whispers, some groans. It seemed as if a lot of men came in, dumped heavy things on the ground, squabbled a long time, then went away. They lay on their hard beds and thought: "This Makola is invaluable." In the morning Carlier came out, very sleepy, and pulled at the cord of the big bell. The station hands mustered every morning to the sound of the bell. That morning nobody came. Kayerts turned out also, yawning. Across the yard they saw Makola come out of his hut, a tin basin of soapy water in his hand. Makola, a civilized nigger, was very neat in his person.

He threw the soapsuds skillfully over a wretched little yellow cur he had, then turning his face to the agent's house, he shouted from the distance, "All the men gone last night!"

They heard him plainly, but in their surprise they both yelled out together: "What!" Then they stared at one another. "We are in a proper fix now," growled Carlier. "It's incredible!" muttered Kayerts. "I will go to the huts and see," said Carlier, striding off.

Makola coming up found Kayerts standing alone.

"I can hardly believe it," said Kayerts, tearfully. "We took care of them as if they had been our children."

"They went with the coast people," said Makola after a moment of hesitation.

"What do I care with whom they went—the ungrateful brutes!" exclaimed the other. Then with sudden suspicion, and looking hard at Makola, he added: "What do you know about it?"

Makola moved his shoulders, looking down on the ground.

"What do I know? I think only. Will you come and look at the ivory I've got there? It is a fine lot. You never saw such."

He moved toward the store. Kayerts followed him mechanically, thinking about the incredible desertion of the men. On the ground before the door of the fetish lay six splendid tusks.

"What did you give for it?" asked Kayerts, after surveying the lot with satisfaction.

"No regular trade," said Makola. "They brought the ivory and gave it to me. I told them to take what they most wanted in the station. It is a beautiful lot. No station can show such tusks. Those traders wanted carriers badly, and our men were no good here. No trade, no entry in books: all correct."

Kayerts nearly burst with indignation. "Why!" he shouted, "I believe you have sold our men for these tusks!" Makola stood impassive and silent. "I—I—will—I," stuttered Kayerts. "You fiend!" he yelled out.

"I did the best for you and the Company," said Makola, imperturbably. "Why you shout so much? Look at this tusk."

"I dismiss you! I will report you—I won't look at the tusk. I forbid you to touch them. I order you to throw them into the river. You—you!"

"You very red, Mr. Kayerts. If you are so irritable in the sun, you will get fever and die—like the first chief!" pronounced Makola impressively.

They stood still, contemplating one another with intense eyes, as if they had been looking with effort across immense distances.

Kayerts shivered. Makola had meant no more than he said, but his words seemed to Kayerts full of ominous menace! He turned sharply and went away to the house. Makola retired into the bosom of his family; and the tusks, left lying before the store, looked very large and valuable in the sunshine.

Carlier came back on the veranda. "They're all gone, hey?" asked Kayerts from the far end of the common room in a muffled voice. "You did not find anybody?"

"Oh, yes," said Carlier, "I found one of Gobila's people lying dead before the huts—shot through the body. We heard that shot last night."

Kayerts came out quickly. He found his companion staring grimly over the yard at the tusks, away by the store. They both sat in silence for a while. Then Kayerts related his conversation with Makola. Carlier said nothing. At the midday meal they ate very little. They hardly exchanged a word that day. A great silence seemed to lie heavily over the station and press on their lips.

Makola did not open the store; he spent the day playing with his children. He lay full-length on a mat outside his door, and the youngsters sat on his chest and clambered all over him. It was a touching picture. Mrs. Makola was busy cooking all day, as usual.

The white men made a somewhat better meal in the evening.

Afterwards, Carlier smoking his pipe strolled over to the store; he stood for a long time over the tusks, touched one or two with his foot, even tried to lift the largest one by its small end. He came back to his chief, who had not stirred from the veranda, threw himself in the chair and said—

"I can see it! They were pounced upon while they slept heavily after drinking all that palm wine you've allowed Makola to give them. A put-up job! See? The worst is, some of Gobila's people were there, and got carried off too, no doubt. The least drunk woke up, and got shot for his sobriety. This is a funny country. What will you do now?"

"We can't touch it, of course," said Kayerts.

"Of course not," assented Carlier.

"Slavery is an awful thing," stammered out Kayerts in an unsteady voice.

"Frightful—the sufferings," grunted Carlier with conviction.

They believed their words. Everybody shows a respectful deference to certain sounds that he and his fellows can make. But about feelings people really know nothing. We talk with indignation or enthusiasm; we talk about oppression, cruelty, crime, devotion, self-sacrifice, virtue, and we know nothing real beyond the words.

Nobody knows what suffering or sacrifice mean—except, perhaps the victims of the mysterious purpose of these illusions.

Next morning they saw Makola very busy setting up in the yard the big scales used for weighing ivory. By and by Carlier said: "What's that filthy scoundrel up to?" and lounged out into the yard. Kayerts followed. They stood watching. Makola took no notice. When the balance was swung true, he tried to lift a tusk into the scale. It was too heavy. He looked up helplessly without a word, and for a minute they stood round that balance as mute and still as three statues. Suddenly Carlier said: "Catch hold of the other end, Makola—you beast!" and together they swung the tusk up. Kayerts trembled in every limb. He muttered, "I say! O! I say!" and putting his hand in his pocket found there a dirty bit of paper and the stump of a pencil. He turned his back on the others, as if about to do something tricky, and noted stealthily the weights which Carlier shouted out to him with unnecessary loudness.

When all was over Makola whispered to himself: "The sun's very strong here for the tusks." Carlier said to Kayerts in a careless tone: "I say, chief, I might just as well give him a lift with this lot into the store."

As they were going back to the house Kayerts observed with a sigh: "It had to be done." And Carlier said: "It's deplorable, but, the men being Company's men the ivory is Company's ivory. We must look after it." "I will report to the Director, of course," said Kayerts. "Of course; let him decide," approved Carlier.

At midday they made a hearty meal. Kayerts sighed from time to time. Whenever they mentioned Makola's name they always added to it an opprobrious epithet. It eased their conscience.

Makola gave himself a half-holiday, and bathed his children in the river. No one from Gobila's villages came near the station that day.

No one came the next day, and the next, nor for a whole week.

Gobila's people might have been dead and buried for any sign of life they gave. But they were only mourning for those they had lost by the witchcraft of white men, who had brought wicked people into their country. The wicked people were gone, but fear remained. Fear always remains. A man may destroy everything within himself, love and hate and belief, and even doubt; but as long as he clings to life he cannot destroy fear: the fear, subtle, indestructible, and terrible, that pervades his being; that tinges his thoughts; that lurks in his heart; that watches on his lips the struggle of his last breath. In his fear, the mild old Gobila offered extra human sacrifices to all the Evil Spirits that had taken possession of his white friends. His heart was heavy. Some warriors spoke about burning and killing, but the cautious old savage dissuaded them.

Who could foresee the woe those mysterious creatures, if irritated, might bring? They should be left alone. Perhaps in time they would disappear into the earth as the first one had disappeared. His people must keep away from them, and hope for the best.

Kayerts and Carlier did not disappear, but remained above on this earth, that, somehow, they fancied had become bigger and very empty. It was not the absolute and dumb solitude of the post that impressed them so much as an inarticulate feeling that something from within them was gone, something that worked for their safety, and had kept the wilderness from interfering with their hearts. The images of home; the memory of people like them, of men that thought and felt as they used to think and feel, receded into distances made indistinct by the glare of unclouded sunshine.

And out of the great silence of the surrounding wilderness, its very hopelessness and savagery seemed to approach them nearer, to draw them gently, to look upon them, to envelop them with a solicitude irresistible, familiar, and disgusting.

Days lengthened into weeks, then into months. Gobila's people drummed and yelled to every new moon, as of yore, but kept away from the station. Makola and Carlier tried once in a canoe to open communications, but were received with a shower of arrows, and had to fly back to the station for dear life. That attempt set the country up and down the river into an uproar that could be very distinctly heard for days. The steamer was late. At first they spoke of delay jauntily, then anxiously, then gloomily. The matter was becoming serious. Stores were running short. Carlier cast his lines off the bank, but the river was low, and the fish kept out in the stream. They dared not stroll far away from the station to shoot.

Moreover, there was no game in the impenetrable forest. Once Carlier shot a hippo in the river. They had no boat to secure it, and it sank. When it floated up it drifted away, and Gobila's people secured the carcass. It was the occasion for a national holiday, but Carlier had a fit of rage over it and talked about the necessity of exterminating all the niggers before the country could be made habitable. Kayerts mooned about silently; spent hours looking at the portrait of his Melie. It represented a little girl with long bleached tresses and a rather sour face. His legs were much swollen, and he could hardly walk. Carlier, undermined by fever, could not swagger any more, but kept tottering about, still with a devil-may-care air, as became a man who remembered his crack regiment. He had become hoarse, sarcastic, and inclined to say unpleasant things.

He called it "being frank with you." They had long ago reckoned their percentages on trade, including in them that last deal of "this infamous Makola." They had also concluded not to say anything about it. Kayerts hesitated at first—was afraid of the Director.

"He has seen worse things done on the quiet," maintained Carlier, with a hoarse laugh. "Trust him! He won't thank you if you blab. He is no better than you or me. Who will talk if we hold our tongues? There is nobody here."

That was the root of the trouble! There was nobody there; and being left there alone with their weakness, they became daily more like a pair of accomplices than like a couple of devoted friends. They had heard nothing from home for eight months. Every evening they said, "Tomorrow we shall see the steamer." But one of the Company's steamers had been wrecked, and the Director was busy with the other, relieving very distant and important stations on the main river. He thought that the useless station, and the useless men, could wait.

Meantime Kayerts and Carlier lived on rice boiled without salt, and cursed the Company, all Africa, and the day they were born. One must have lived on such diet to discover what ghastly trouble the necessity of swallowing one's food may become.

There was literally nothing else in the station but rice and coffee; they drank the coffee without sugar. The last fifteen lumps Kayerts had solemnly locked away in his box, together with a half-bottle of cognac, "in case of sickness," he explained.

Carlier approved. "When one is sick," he said, "any little extra like that is cheering."

They waited. Rank grass began to sprout over the courtyard.

The bell never rang now. Days passed, silent, exasperating, and slow. When the two men spoke, they snarled; and their silences were bitter, as if tinged by the bitterness of their thoughts.

One day after a lunch of boiled rice, Carlier put down his cup untasted, and said: "Hang it all! Let's have a decent cup of coffee for once. Bring out that sugar, Kayerts!" "For the sick," muttered Kayerts, without looking up.

"For the sick," mocked Carlier. "Bosh! . . . Well! I am sick." "You are no more sick than I am, and I go without," said Kayerts in a peaceful tone.

"Come! out with that sugar, you stingy old slave-dealer."

Kayerts looked up quickly. Carlier was smiling with marked insolence. And suddenly it seemed to Kayerts that he had never seen that man before. Who was he? He knew nothing about him.

What was he capable of? There was a surprising flash of violent emotion within him, as if in the presence of something undreamt of, dangerous, and final. But he managed to pronounce with composure—

"That joke is in very bad taste. Don't repeat it."

"Joke!" said Carlier, hitching himself forward on his seat. "I am hungry—I am sick—I don't joke! I hate hypocrites. You are a hypocrite. You are a slave-dealer. I am a slave-dealer. There's nothing but slave-dealers in this cursed country. I mean to have sugar in my coffee today, anyhow!"

"I forbid you to speak to me in that way," said Kayerts with a fair show of resolution.

"You!—What?" shouted Carlier, jumping up.

Kayerts stood up also. "I am your chief," he began, trying to master the shakiness of his voice.

"What?" yelled the other. "Who's chief? There's no chief here. There's nothing here: there's nothing but you and I. Fetch the sugar—you pot-bellied ass."

"Hold your tongue. Go out of this room," screamed Kayerts. "I dismiss you—you scoundrel!"

Carlier swung a stool. All at once he looked dangerously in earnest. "You flabby, good-for-nothing civilian—take that!" he howled.

Kayerts dropped under the table, and the stool struck the grass inner wall of the room. Then, as Carlier was trying to upset the table, Kayerts in desperation made a blind rush, head low, like a cornered pig would do, and over-turning his friend, bolted along the veranda, and into his room. He locked the door, snatched his revolver, and stood panting. In less than a minute Carlier was kicking at the door furiously, howling, "If you don't bring out that sugar, I will shoot you at sight, like a dog. Now then—one—two—three. You won't? I will show you who's the master."

Kayerts thought the door would fall in, and scrambled through the square hole that served for a window in his room. There was then the whole breadth of the house between them. But the other was apparently not strong enough to break in the door, and Kayerts heard him running round. Then he also began to run laboriously on his swollen legs. He ran as quickly as he could, grasping the revolver, and unable yet to understand what was happening to him. He saw in succession Makola's house, the store, the river, the ravine, and the low bushes; and he saw all those things again as he ran for the second time round the house. Then again they flashed past him. That morning he could not have walked a yard without a groan.

And now he ran. He ran fast enough to keep out of sight of the other man.

Then as, weak and desperate, he thought, "Before I finish the next round I shall die," he heard the other man stumble heavily, then stop. He stopped also. He had the back and Carlier the front of the house, as before. He heard him drop into a chair cursing, and suddenly his own legs gave way, and he slid down into a sitting posture with his back to the wall. His mouth was as dry as a cinder, and his face was wet with perspiration—and tears. What was it all about? He thought it must be a horrible illusion; he thought he was dreaming; he thought he was going mad! After a while he collected his senses. What did they quarrel about? That sugar! How absurd! He would give it to him—didn't want it himself. And he began scrambling to his feet with a sudden feeling of security. But before he had fairly stood upright, a commonsense reflection occurred to him and drove him back into despair. He thought: "If I give way now to that brute of a soldier, he will begin this horror again tomorrow—and the day after—every day—raise other pretensions, trample on me, torture me, make me his slave—and I will be lost! Lost! The steamer may not come for days—may never come." He shook so that he had to sit down on the floor again. He shivered forlornly. He felt he could not, would not move any more. He was completely distracted by the sudden perception that the position was without issue—that death and life had in a moment become equally difficult and terrible.

All at once he heard the other push his chair back; and he leaped to his feet with extreme facility. He listened and got confused.

Must run again! Right or left? He heard footsteps. He darted to the left, grasping his revolver, and at the very same instant, as it seemed to him, they came into violent collision. Both shouted with surprise.

A loud explosion took place between them; a roar of red fire, thick smoke; and Kayerts, deafened and blinded, rushed back thinking: "I am hit—it's all over." He expected the other to come round—to gloat over his agony. He caught hold of an upright of the roof—"All over!" Then he heard a crashing fall on the other side of the house, as if somebody had tumbled headlong over a chair—then silence. Nothing more happened. He did not die.

Only his shoulder felt as if it had been badly wrenched, and he had lost his revolver. He was disarmed and helpless! He waited for his fate. The other man made no sound. It was a stratagem. He was stalking him now! Along what side? Perhaps he was taking aim this very minute!

After a few moments of an agony frightful and absurd, he decided to go and meet his doom. He was prepared for every surrender.

He turned the corner, steadying himself with one hand on the wall; made a few paces, and nearly swooned. He had seen on the floor, protruding past the other corner, a pair of turned-up feet. A pair of white naked feet in red slippers. He felt deadly sick, and stood for a time in profound darkness. Then Makola appeared before him, saying quietly: "Come along, Mr. Kayerts. He is dead." He burst into tears of gratitude; a loud, sobbing fit of crying.

After a time he found himself sitting in a chair and looking at Carlier, who lay stretched on his back. Makola was kneeling over the body.

"Is this your revolver?" asked Makola, getting up.

"Yes," said Kayerts; then he added very quickly, "He ran after me to shoot me—you saw!" "Yes, I saw," said Makola. "There is only one revolver; where's his?"

"Don't know," whispered Kayerts in a voice that had become suddenly very faint.

"I will go and look for it," said the other, gently. He made the round along the veranda, while Kayerts sat still and looked at the corpse. Makola came back empty-handed, stood in deep thought, then stepped quietly into the dead man's room, and came out directly with a revolver, which he held up before Kayerts. Kayerts shut his eyes. Everything was going round. He found life more terrible and difficult than death. He had shot an unarmed man.

After meditating for a while, Makola said softly, pointing at the dead man who lay there with his right eye blown out—

"He died of fever." Kayerts looked at him with a stony stare.

"Yes," repeated Makola, thoughtfully, stepping over the corpse, "I think he died of fever. Bury him tomorrow."

And he went away slowly to his expectant wife, leaving the two white men alone on the veranda.

Night came, and Kayerts sat unmoving on his chair. He sat quiet as if he had taken a dose of opium. The violence of the emotions he had passed through produced a feeling of exhausted serenity.

He had plumbed in one short afternoon the depths of horror and despair, and now found repose in the conviction that life had no more secrets for him: neither had death! He sat by the corpse thinking; thinking very actively, thinking very new thoughts. He seemed to have broken loose from himself altogether. His old thoughts, convictions, likes and dislikes, things he respected and things he abhorred, appeared in their true light at last! Appeared contemptible and childish, false and ridiculous. He reveled in his new wisdom while he sat by the man he had killed. He argued with himself about all things under heaven with that kind of wrong-headed lucidity which may be observed in some lunatics.

Incidentally he reflected that the fellow dead there had been a noxious beast anyway; that men died every day in thousands; perhaps in hundreds of thousands—who could tell?—and that in the number, that one death could not possibly make any difference; couldn't have any importance, at least to a thinking creature. He, Kayerts, was a thinking creature. He had been all his life, till that moment, a believer in a lot of nonsense like the rest of mankind—who are fools; but now he thought! He knew! He was at peace; he was familiar with the highest wisdom! Then he tried to imagine himself dead, and Carlier sitting in his chair watching him; and his attempt met with such unexpected success, that in a very few moments he became not at all sure who was dead and who was alive. This extraordinary achievement of his fancy startled him, however, and by a clever and timely effort of mind he saved himself just in time from becoming Carlier. His heart thumped, and he felt hot all over at the thought of that danger. Carlier! What a beastly thing! To compose his now disturbed nerves—and no wonder!—he tried to whistle a little. Then, suddenly, he fell asleep, or thought he had slept; but at any rate there was a fog, and somebody had whistled in the fog.

He stood up. The day had come, and a heavy mist had descended upon the land: the mist penetrating, enveloping, and silent; the morning mist of tropical lands; the mist that clings and kills; the mist white and deadly, immaculate and poisonous. He stood up, saw the body, and threw his arms above his head with a cry like that of a man who, waking from a trance, finds himself immured forever in a tomb. "Help! . . . . My God!"

A shriek inhuman, vibrating and sudden, pierced like a sharp dart the white shroud of that land of sorrow. Three short, impatient screeches followed, and then, for a time, the fog-wreaths rolled on, undisturbed, through a formidable silence. Then many more shrieks, rapid and piercing, like the yells of some exasperated and ruthless creature, rent the air. Progress was calling to Kayerts from the river. Progress and civilization and all the virtues. Society was calling to its accomplished child to come, to be taken care of, to be instructed, to be judged, to be condemned; it called him to return to that rubbish heap from which he had wandered away, so that justice could be done.

Kayerts heard and understood. He stumbled out of the veranda, leaving the other man quite alone for the first time since they had been thrown there together. He groped his way through the fog, calling in his ignorance upon the invisible heaven to undo its work. Makola flitted by in the mist, shouting as he ran—

"Steamer! Steamer! They can't see. They whistle for the station. I go ring the bell. Go down to the landing, sir. I ring."

He disappeared. Kayerts stood still. He looked upwards; the fog rolled low over his head. He looked round like a man who has lost his way; and he saw a dark smudge, a cross-shaped stain, upon the shifting purity of the mist. As he began to stumble toward it, the station bell rang in a tumultuous peal its answer to the impatient clamor of the steamer.

The Managing Director of the Great Civilizing Company (since we know that civilization follows trade) landed first, and incontinently lost sight of the steamer. The fog down by the river was exceedingly dense; above, at the station, the bell rang unceasing and brazen.

The Director shouted loudly to the steamer:

"There is nobody down to meet us; there may be something wrong, though they are ringing. You had better come, too!" And he began to toil up the steep bank. The captain and the engine-driver of the boat followed behind. As they scrambled up the fog thinned, and they could see their Director a good way ahead. Suddenly they saw him start forward, calling to them over his shoulder:—"Run! Run to the house! I've found one of them. Run, look for the other!"

He had found one of them! And even he, the man of varied and startling experience, was somewhat discomposed by the manner of this finding. He stood and fumbled in his pockets (for a knife) while he faced Kayerts, who was hanging by a leather strap from the cross. He had evidently climbed the grave, which was high and narrow, and after tying the end of the strap to the arm, had swung himself off. His toes were only a couple of inches above the ground; his arms hung stiffly down; he seemed to be standing rigidly at attention, but with one purple cheek playfully posed on the shoulder. And, irreverently, he was putting out a swollen tongue at his Managing Director.

AN ANARCHIST

A Desperate Tale

THAT YEAR I spent the best two months of the dry season on one of the estates—in fact, on the principal cattle estate—of a famous meat-extract manufacturing company.

B.O.S. Bos. You have seen the three magic letters on the advertisement pages of magazines and newspapers, in the windows of provision merchants, and on calendars for next year you receive by post in the month of November. They scatter pamphlets also, written in a sickly enthusiastic style and in several languages, giving statistics of slaughter and bloodshed enough to make a Turk turn faint. The "art" illustrating that "literature" represents in vivid and shining colors a large and enraged black bull stamping upon a yellow snake writhing in emerald-green grass, with a cobalt-blue sky for a background. It is atrocious and it is an allegory. The snake symbolizes disease, weakness—perhaps mere hunger, which last is the chronic disease of the majority of mankind. Of course everybody knows the B. O. S. Ltd., with its unrivalled products: Vinobos, Jellybos, and the latest unequalled perfection, Tribos, whose nourishment is offered to you not only highly concentrated, but already half digested. Such apparently is the love that Limited Company bears to its fellowmen—even as the love of the father and mother penguin for their hungry fledglings.

Of course the capital of a country must be productively employed. I have nothing to say against the company. But being myself animated by feelings of affection toward my fellow-men, I am saddened by the modern system of advertising. Whatever evidence it offers of enterprise, ingenuity, impudence, and resource in certain individuals, it proves to my mind the wide prevalence of that form of mental degradation which is called gullibility.

In various parts of the civilized and uncivilized world I have had to swallow B. O. S. with more or less benefit to myself, though without great pleasure. Prepared with hot water and abundantly peppered to bring out the taste, this extract is not really unpalatable.

But I have never swallowed its advertisements. Perhaps they have not gone far enough. As far as I can remember they make no promise of everlasting youth to the users of B. O. S., nor yet have they claimed the power of raising the dead for their estimable products. Why this austere reserve, I wonder? But I don't think they would have had me even on these terms. Whatever form of mental degradation I may (being but human) be suffering from, it is not the popular form. I am not gullible.

I have been at some pains to bring out distinctly this statement about myself in view of the story which follows. I have checked the facts as far as possible. I have turned up the files of French newspapers, and I have also talked with the officer who commands the military guard on the *Ile Royale*, when in the course of my travels I reached Cayenne. I believe the story to be in the main true. It is the sort of story that no man, I think, would ever invent about himself, for it is neither grandiose nor flattering, nor yet funny enough to gratify a perverted vanity.

It concerns the engineer of the steam-launch belonging to the Marañon cattle estate of the B. O. S. Co., Ltd. This estate is also an island—an island as big as a small province, lying in the estuary of a great South American river. It is wild and not beautiful, but the grass growing on its low plains seems to possess exceptionally nourishing and flavoring qualities. It resounds with the lowing of innumerable herds—a deep and distressing sound under the open sky, rising like a monstrous protest of prisoners condemned to death. On the mainland, across twenty miles of discolored muddy water, there stands a city whose name, let us say, is Horta.

But the most interesting characteristic of this island (which seems like a sort of penal settlement for condemned cattle) consists in its being the only known habitat of an extremely rare and gorgeous butterfly. The species is even more rare than it is beautiful, which is not saying little. I have already alluded to my travels. I traveled at that time, but strictly for myself and with a moderation unknown in our days of round-the-world tickets. I even traveled with a purpose. As a matter of fact, I am—"Ha, ha, ha!—a desperate butterfly-slayer. Ha, ha, ha!"

This was the tone in which Mr. Harry Gee, the manager of the cattle station, alluded to my pursuits. He seemed to consider me the greatest absurdity in the world. On the other hand, the B. O. S. Co., Ltd., represented to him the acme of the nineteenth century's achievement. I believe that he slept in his leggings and spurs. His days he spent in the saddle flying over the plains, followed by a train of half-wild horsemen, who called him Don Enrique, and who had no definite idea of the B. O. S. Co., Ltd., which paid their wages. He was an excellent manager, but I don't see why, when we met at meals, he should have thumped me on the back, with loud, derisive inquiries: "How's the deadly sport today? Butterflies going strong? Ha, ha, ha!"—especially as he charged me two dollars per diem for the hospitality of the B. O. S. Co., Ltd., (capital £1,500,000, fully paid up), in whose balance sheet for that year those monies are no doubt included. "I don't think I can make it anything less in justice to my company," he had remarked, with extreme gravity, when I was arranging with him the terms of my stay on the island.

His chaff would have been harmless enough if intimacy of intercourse in the absence of all friendly feeling were not a thing detestable in itself. Moreover, his facetiousness was not very amusing. It consisted in the wearisome repetition of descriptive phrases applied to people with a burst of laughter. "Desperate butterfly-slayer. Ha, ha, ha!" was one sample of his peculiar wit which he himself enjoyed so much. And in the same vein of exquisite humor he called my attention to the engineer of the steam-launch, one day, as we strolled on the path by the side of the creek.

The man's head and shoulders emerged above the deck, over which were scattered various tools of his trade and a few pieces of machinery. He was doing some repairs to the engines. At the sound of our footsteps he raised anxiously a grimy face with a pointed chin and a tiny fair mustache. What could be seen of his delicate features under the black smudges appeared to me wasted and livid in the greenish shade of the enormous tree spreading its foliage over the launch moored close to the bank.

To my great surprise, Harry Gee addressed him as "Crocodile," in that half-jeering, half-bullying tone which is characteristic of self-satisfaction in his delectable kind:

"How does the work get on, Crocodile?"

I should have said before that the amiable Harry had picked up French of a sort somewhere—in some colony or other—and that he pronounced it with a disagreeable forced precision as though he meant to guy the language. The man in the launch answered him quickly in a pleasant voice. His eyes had a liquid softness and his teeth flashed dazzlingly white between his thin, drooping lips. The manager turned to me, very cheerful and loud, explaining:

"I call him Crocodile because he lives half in, half out of the creek. Amphibious—see? There's nothing else amphibious living on the island except crocodiles; so he must belong to the species—eh? But in reality he's nothing less than *un citoyen anarchiste de Barcelone.*"

"A citizen anarchist from Barcelona?" I repeated, stupidly, looking down at the man. He had turned to his work in the engine well of the launch and presented his bowed back to us. In that attitude I heard him protest, very audibly:

"I do not even know Spanish."

"Hey? What? You dare to deny you come from over there?" the accomplished manager was down on him truculently.

At this the man straightened himself up, dropping a spanner he had been using, and faced us; but he trembled in all his limbs.

"I deny nothing, nothing, nothing!" he said, excitedly.

He picked up the spanner and went to work again without paying any further attention to us. After looking at him for a minute or so, we went away.

"Is he really an anarchist?" I asked, when out of ear-shot.

"I don't care a hang what he is," answered the humorous official of the B. O. S. Co. "I gave him the name because it suited me to label him in that way, it's good for the company."

"For the company!" I exclaimed, stopping short.

"Aha!" he triumphed, tilting up his hairless pug face and straddling his thin, long legs. "That surprises you. I am bound to do my best for my company. They have enormous expenses. Why—our agent in Horta tells me they spend fifty thousand pounds every year in advertising all over the world! One can't be too economical in working the show. Well, just you listen. When I took charge here the estate had no steam-launch. I asked for one, and kept on asking by every mail till I got it; but the man they sent out with it chucked his job at the end of two months, leaving the launch moored at the pontoon in Horta. Got a better screw at a sawmill up the river—blast him! And ever since it has been the same thing. Any Scotch or Yankee vagabond that likes to call himself a mechanic out here gets eighteen pounds a month, and the next you know he's cleared out, after smashing something as likely as not. I give you my word that some of the objects I've had for engine-drivers couldn't tell the boiler from the funnel. But this fellow understands his trade, and I don't mean him to clear out. See?"

And he struck me lightly on the chest for emphasis. Disregarding his peculiarities of manner, I wanted to know what all this had to do with the man being an anarchist.

"Come!" jeered the manager. "If you saw suddenly a barefooted, unkempt chap slinking among the bushes on the sea face of the island,

and at the same time observed less than a mile from the beach, a small schooner full of niggers hauling off in a hurry, you wouldn't think the man fell there from the sky, would you? And it could be nothing else but either that or Cayenne. I've got my wits about me. Directly I sighted this queer game I said to myself—'Escaped Convict.' I was as certain of it as I am of seeing you standing here this minute. So I spurred on straight at him. He stood his ground for a bit on a sand hillock crying out: '*Monsieur! Monsieur! Arrêtez!*' then at the last moment broke and ran for life.

"Says I to myself, 'I'll tame you before I'm done with you.' So without a single word I kept on, heading him off here and there. I rounded him up toward the shore, and at last I had him corralled on a spit, his heels in the water and nothing but sea and sky at his back, with my horse pawing the sand and shaking his head within a yard of him.

"He folded his arms on his breast then and stuck his chin up in a sort of desperate way; but I wasn't to be impressed by the beggar's posturing.

"Says I, 'You're a runaway convict.'"

When he heard French, his chin went down and his face changed.

"'I deny nothing,' says he, panting yet, for I had kept him skipping about in front of my horse pretty smartly. I asked him what he was doing there. He had got his breath by then, and explained that he had meant to make his way to a farm which he understood (from the schooner's people, I suppose) was to be found in the neighborhood. At that I laughed aloud and he got uneasy. Had he been deceived? Was there no farm within walking distance?"

"I laughed more and more. He was on foot, and of course the first bunch of cattle he came across would have stamped him to rags under their hoofs. A dismounted man caught on the feeding grounds hasn't got the ghost of a chance.

"'My coming upon you like this has certainly saved your life,' I said. He remarked that perhaps it was so; but that for his part he had imagined I had wanted to kill him under the hoofs of my horse. I assured him that nothing would have been easier had I meant it. And then we came to a sort of dead stop. For the life of me I didn't know what to do with this convict, unless I chucked him into the sea. It occurred to me to ask him what he had been transported for. He hung his head.

"'What is it?' says I. 'Theft, murder, rape, or what?' I wanted to hear what he would have to say for himself, though of course I expected it would be some sort of lie. But all he said was—"

"'Make it what you like. I deny nothing. It is no good denying anything.'" I looked him over carefully and a thought struck me.

"'They've got anarchists there, too,' I said. 'Perhaps you're one of them.'"

"I deny nothing whatever, monsieur,' he repeats.

"This answer made me think that perhaps he was not an anarchist. I believe those damned lunatics are rather proud of themselves. If he had been one, he would have probably confessed straight out.

"'What were you before you became a convict?'"

"'*Ouvrier*,' he says. 'And a good workman, too.'

"At that I began to think he must be an anarchist, after all.

"That's the class they come mostly from, isn't it? I hate the cowardly bomb-throwing brutes. I almost made up my mind to turn my horse short round and leave him to starve or drown where he was, whichever he liked best. As to crossing the island to bother me again, the cattle would see to that. I don't know what induced me to ask—

"'What sort of workman?'"

"I didn't care a hang whether he answered me or not. But when he said at once, '*Mécanicien, monsieur*,' I nearly jumped out of the saddle with excitement. The launch had been lying disabled and idle in the creek for three weeks. My duty to the company was clear. He noticed my start, too, and there we were for a minute or so staring at each other as if bewitched.

"'Get up on my horse behind me,' I told him. 'You shall put my steam-launch to rights.'"

These are the words in which the worthy manager of the Marañon estate related to me the coming of the supposed anarchist. He meant to keep him—out of a sense of duty to the company—and the name he had given him would prevent the fellow from obtaining employment anywhere in Horta. The vaqueros of the estate, when they went on leave, spread it all over the town. They did not know what an anarchist was, nor yet what Barcelona meant.

They called him Anarchisto de Barcelona, as if it were his Christian name and surname. But the people in town had been reading in their papers about the anarchists in Europe and were very much impressed. Over the jocular addition of "de Barcelona" Mr. Harry Gee chuckled with immense satisfaction. "That breed is particularly murderous, isn't it? It makes the sawmills crowd still more afraid of having anything to do with him—see?" he exulted, candidly.

"I hold him by that name better than if I had him chained up by the leg to the deck of the steam-launch.

"And mark," he added, after a pause, "he does not deny it. I am not wronging him in any way. He is a convict of some sort, anyhow."

"But I suppose you pay him some wages, don't you?" I asked.

"Wages! What does he want with money here? He gets his food from my kitchen and his clothing from the store. Of course I'll give him something at the end of the year, but you don't think I'd employ a convict and give him the same money I would give an honest man? I am looking after the interests of my company first and last."

I admitted that, for a company spending fifty thousand pounds every year in advertising, the strictest economy was obviously necessary.

The manager of the Marañon Estancia grunted approvingly.

"And I'll tell you what," he continued: "if I were certain he's an anarchist and he had the cheek to ask me for money, I would give him the toe of my boot. However, let him have the benefit of the doubt. I am perfectly willing to take it that he has done nothing worse than to stick a knife into somebody—with extenuating circumstances—French fashion, don't you know. But that subversive sanguinary rot of doing away with all law and order in the world makes my blood boil. It's simply cutting the ground from under the feet of every decent, respectable, hard-working person. I tell you that the consciences of people who have them, like you or I, must be protected in some way; or else the first low scoundrel that came along would in every respect be just as good as myself. Wouldn't he, now? And that's absurd!" He glared at me. I nodded slightly and murmured that doubtless there was much subtle truth in his view.

The principal truth discoverable in the views of Paul the engineer was that a little thing may bring about the undoing of a man.

"*Il ne faut pas beaucoup pour perdre un homme*," he said to me, thoughtfully, one evening.

I report this reflection in French, since the man was of Paris, not of Barcelona at all. At the Marañon he lived apart from the station, in a small shed with a metal roof and straw walls, which he called *mon atelier*. He had a work-bench there. They had given him several horse-blankets and a saddle—not that he ever had occasion to ride, but because no other bedding was used by the working-hands, who were all vaqueros—cattlemen. And on this horseman's gear, like a son of the plains, he used to sleep among the tools of his trade, in a litter of rusty scrap-iron, with a portable forge at his head, under the work-bench sustaining his grimy mosquito-net.

Now and then I would bring him a few candle ends saved from the scant supply of the manager's house. He was very thankful for these. He did not like to lie awake in the dark, he confessed. He complained that sleep fled from him. "*Le sommeil me fuit*," he declared, with his habitual air of subdued stoicism, which made him sympathetic and touching. I made it clear to him that I did not attach undue importance to the fact of his having been a convict.

Thus it came about that one evening he was led to talk about himself. As one of the bits of candle on the edge of the bench burned down to the end, he hastened to light another.

He had done his military service in a provincial garrison and returned to Paris to follow his trade. It was a well-paid one. He told me with some pride that in a short time he was earning no less than ten francs a day. He was thinking of setting up for himself by and by and of getting married.

Here he sighed deeply and paused. Then with a return to his stoical note:

"It seems I did not know enough about myself."

On his twenty-fifth birthday two of his friends in the repairing shop where he worked proposed to stand him a dinner. He was immensely touched by this attention.

"I was a steady man," he remarked, "but I am not less sociable than any other body."

The entertainment came off in a little café on the Boulevard de la Chapelle. At dinner they drank some special wine. It was excellent.

Everything was excellent; and the world—in his own words—seemed a very good place to live in. He had good prospects, some little money laid by, and the affection of two excellent friends. He offered to pay for all the drinks after dinner, which was only proper on his part.

They drank more wine; they drank liqueurs, cognac, beer, then more liqueurs and more cognac. Two strangers sitting at the next table looked at him, he said, with so much friendliness, that he invited them to join the party.

He had never drunk so much in his life. His elation was extreme, and so pleasurable that whenever it flagged he hastened to order more drinks.

"It seemed to me," he said, in his quiet tone and looking on the ground in the gloomy shed full of shadows, "that I was on the point of just attaining a great and wonderful felicity. Another drink, I felt, would do it. The others were holding out well with me, glass for glass."

But an extraordinary thing happened. At something the strangers said his elation fell. Gloomy ideas—*des idées noires*—rushed into his head. All the world outside the café; appeared to him as a dismal evil place where a multitude of poor wretches had to work and slave to the sole end that a few individuals should ride in carriages and live riotously in palaces. He became ashamed of his happiness. The pity of mankind's cruel lot wrung his heart. In a voice choked with sorrow he tried to express these sentiments. He thinks he wept and swore in turns.

The two new acquaintances hastened to applaud his humane indignation. Yes. The amount of injustice in the world was indeed scandalous. There was only one way of dealing with the rotten state of society. Demolish the whole *sacrée boutique*. Blow up the whole iniquitous show.

Their heads hovered over the table. They whispered to him eloquently; I don't think they quite expected the result. He was extremely drunk—mad drunk. With a howl of rage he leaped suddenly upon the table. Kicking over the bottles and glasses, he yelled: "*Vive l'anarchie!* Death to the capitalists!" He yelled this again and again. All round him broken glass was falling, chairs were being swung in the air, people were taking each other by the throat. The police dashed in. He hit, bit, scratched and struggled, till something crashed down upon his head. . . .

He came to himself in a police cell, locked up on a charge of assault, seditious cries, and anarchist propaganda.

He looked at me fixedly with his liquid, shining eyes, that seemed very big in the dim light.

"That was bad. But even then I might have got off somehow, perhaps," he said, slowly.

I doubt it. But whatever chance he had was done away with by a young socialist lawyer who volunteered to undertake his defense.

In vain he assured him that he was no anarchist; that he was a quiet, respectable mechanic, only too anxious to work ten hours per day at his trade. He was represented at the trial as the victim of society and his drunken shoutings as the expression of infinite suffering.

The young lawyer had his way to make, and this case was just what he wanted for a start. The speech for the defense was pronounced magnificent.

The poor fellow paused, swallowed, and brought out the statement:

"I got the maximum penalty applicable to a first offence."

I made an appropriate murmur. He hung his head and folded his arms.

"When they let me out of prison," he began, gently, "I made tracks, of course, for my old workshop. My *patron* had a particular liking for me before; but when he saw me he turned green with fright and showed me the door with a shaking hand."

While he stood in the street, uneasy and disconcerted, he was accosted by a middle-aged man who introduced himself as an engineer's fitter, too. "I know who you are," he said. "I have attended your trial. You are a good comrade and your ideas are sound. But the devil of it is that you won't be able to get work anywhere now. These bourgeois'll conspire to starve you. That's their way. Expect no mercy from the rich."

To be spoken to so kindly in the street had comforted him very much. His seemed to be the sort of nature needing support and sympathy. The idea of not being able to find work had knocked him over completely. If his *patron,* who knew him so well for a quiet, orderly, competent workman, would have nothing to do with him now—then surely nobody else would. That was clear.

The police, keeping their eye on him, would hasten to warn every employer inclined to give him a chance. He felt suddenly very helpless, alarmed, and idle; and he followed the middle-aged man to the estaminet round the corner where he met some other good companions. They assured him that he would not be allowed to starve, work or no work. They had drinks all round to the discomfiture of all employers of labor and to the destruction of society.

He sat biting his lower lip.

"That is, monsieur, how I became a *compagnon,*" he said. The hand he passed over his forehead was trembling. "All the same, there's something wrong in a world where a man can get lost for a glass more or less."

He never looked up, though I could see he was getting excited under his dejection. He slapped the bench with his open palm.

"No!" he cried. "It was an impossible existence! Watched by the police, watched by the comrades, I did not belong to myself any more! Why, I could not even go to draw a few francs from my savings-bank without a comrade hanging about the door to see that I didn't bolt! And most of them were neither more nor less than housebreakers. The intelligent, I mean. They robbed the rich; they were only getting back their own, they said. When I had had some drink I believed them. There were also the fools and the mad. *Des exaltes—quoi!* When I was drunk I loved them. When I got more drink I was angry with the world. That was the best time. I found refuge from misery in rage. But one can't be always drunk—*n'est-ce pas, monsieur*? And when I was sober I was afraid to break away. They would have stuck me like a pig."

He folded his arms again and raised his sharp chin with a bitter smile.

"By and by they told me it was time to go to work. The work was to rob a bank. Afterwards a bomb would be thrown to wreck the place. My beginner's part would be to keep watch in a street at the back and to take care of a black bag with the bomb inside till it was wanted. After the meeting at which the affair was arranged a trusty comrade did not leave me an inch. I had not dared to protest; I was afraid of being done away with quietly in that room; only, as we were walking together I wondered whether it would not be better for me to throw myself suddenly into the Seine. But while I was turning it over in my mind we had crossed the bridge, and afterwards I had not the opportunity."

In the light of the candle end, with his sharp features, fluffy little mustache, and oval face, he looked at times delicately and gaily young, and then appeared quite old, decrepit, full of sorrow, pressing his folded arms to his breast.

As he remained silent I felt bound to ask:

"Well! And how did it end?"

"Deportation to Cayenne," he answered.

He seemed to think that somebody had given the plot away. As he was keeping watch in the back street, bag in hand, he was set upon by the police. "These imbeciles," had knocked him down without noticing what he had in his hand. He wondered how the bomb failed to explode as he fell. But it didn't explode.

"I tried to tell my story in court," he continued. "The president was amused. There were in the audience some idiots who laughed."

I expressed the hope that some of his companions had been caught, too. He shuddered slightly before he told me that there were two—Simon, called also Biscuit, the middle-aged fitter who spoke to him in the street, and a fellow of the name of Mafile, one of the sympathetic strangers who had applauded his sentiments and consoled his humanitarian sorrows when he got drunk in the café.

"Yes," he went on, with an effort, "I had the advantage of their company over there on St. Joseph's Island, among some eighty or ninety other convicts. We were all classed as dangerous."

St. Joseph's Island is the prettiest of the *Iles de Salut*. It is rocky and green, with shallow ravines, bushes, thickets, groves of mango-trees, and many feathery palms. Six warders armed with revolvers and carbines are in charge of the convicts kept there.

An eight-oared galley keeps up the communication in the day time, across a channel a quarter of a mile wide, with the *Ile Royale*, where there is a military post. She makes the first trip at six in the morning. At four in the afternoon her service is over, and she is then hauled up into a little dock on the *Ile Royale* and a sentry put over her and a few smaller boats. From that time till next morning the island of St. Joseph remains cut off from the rest of the world, with the warders patrolling in turn the path from the warders' house to the convict huts, and a multitude of sharks patrolling the waters all round.

Under these circumstances the convicts planned a mutiny. Such a thing had never been known in the penitentiary's history before.

But their plan was not without some possibility of success. The warders were to be taken by surprise and murdered during the night. Their arms would enable the convicts to shoot down the people in the galley as she came alongside in the morning. The galley once in their possession, other boats were to be captured, and the whole company was to row away up the coast.

At dusk the two warders on duty mustered the convicts as usual. Then they proceeded to inspect the huts to ascertain that everything was in order. In the second they entered they were set upon and absolutely smothered under the numbers of their assailants.

The twilight faded rapidly. It was a new moon; and a heavy black squall gathering over the coast increased the profound darkness of the night. The convicts assembled in the open space, deliberating upon the next step to be taken, argued among themselves in low voices.

"You took part in all this?" I asked.

"No. I knew what was going to be done, of course. But why should I kill these warders? I had nothing against them. But I was afraid of the others. Whatever happened, I could not escape from them. I sat alone on the stump of a tree with my head in my hands, sick at heart at the thought of a freedom that could be nothing but a mockery to me. Suddenly I was startled to perceive the shape of a man on the path near by. He stood perfectly still, then his form became effaced in the night. It must have been the chief warder coming to see what had become of his two men. No one noticed him. The convicts kept on quarreling over their plans. The leaders could not get themselves obeyed. The fierce whispering of that dark mass of men was very horrible.

"At last they divided into two parties and moved off. When they had passed me I rose, weary and hopeless. The path to the warders' house was dark and silent, but on each side the bushes rustled slightly. Presently I saw a faint thread of light before me. The chief warder, followed by his three men, was approaching cautiously.

But he had failed to close his dark lantern properly. The convicts had seen that faint gleam, too. There was an awful savage yell, a turmoil on the dark path, shots fired, blows, groans: and with the sound of smashed bushes, the shouts of the pursuers and the screams of the pursued, the man-hunt, the warder-hunt, passed by me into the interior of the island. I was alone. And I assure you, monsieur, I was indifferent to everything. After standing still for a while, I walked on along the path till I kicked something hard. I stooped and picked up a warder's revolver. I felt with my fingers that it was loaded in five chambers. In the gusts of wind I heard the convicts calling to each other far away, and then a roll of thunder would cover the soughing and rustling of the trees. Suddenly, a big light ran across my path very low along the ground. And it showed a woman's skirt with the edge of an apron.

"I knew that the person who carried it must be the wife of the head warder. They had forgotten all about her, it seems. A shot rang out in the interior of the island, and she cried out to herself as she ran. She passed on. I followed, and presently I saw her again. She was pulling at the cord of the big bell which hangs at the end of the landing-pier, with one hand, and with the other she was swinging the heavy lantern to and fro. This is the agreed signal for the *Ile Royale* should assistance be required at night. The wind carried the sound away from our island and the light she swung was hidden on the shore side by the few trees that grow near the warders' house.

"I came up quite close to her from behind. She went on without stopping, without looking aside, as though she had been all alone on the island. A brave woman, monsieur. I put the revolver inside the breast of my blue blouse and waited. A flash of lightning and a clap of thunder destroyed both the sound and the light of the signal for an instant, but she never faltered, pulling at the cord and swinging the lantern as regularly as a machine. She was a comely woman of thirty—no more. I thought to myself, 'All that's no good on a night like this.' And I made up my mind that if a body of my fellow-convicts came down to the pier—which was sure to happen soon—I would shoot her through the head before I shot myself. I knew the 'comrades' well. This idea of mine gave me quite an interest in life, monsieur; and at once, instead of remaining stupidly exposed on the pier, I retreated a little way and crouched behind a bush. I did not intend to let myself be pounced upon unawares and be prevented perhaps from rendering a supreme service to at least one human creature before I died myself.

"But we must believe the signal was seen, for the galley from *Ile Royale* came over in an astonishingly short time. The woman kept right on till the light of her lantern flashed upon the officer in command and the bayonets of the soldiers in the boat. Then she sat down and began to cry.

"She didn't need me any more. I did not budge. Some soldiers were only in their shirt-sleeves, others without boots, just as the call to arms had found them. They passed by my bush at the double. The galley had been sent away for more; and the woman sat all alone crying at the end of the pier, with the lantern standing on the ground near her.

"Then suddenly I saw in the light at the end of the pier the red pantaloons of two more men. I was overcome with astonishment.

They, too, started off at a run. Their tunics flapped unbuttoned and they were bare-headed. One of them panted out to the other, 'Straight on, straight on!'

"Where on earth did they spring from, I wondered. Slowly I walked down the short pier. I saw the woman's form shaken by sobs and heard her moaning more and more distinctly, 'Oh, my man! my poor man! my poor man!' I stole on quietly. She could neither hear nor see anything. She had thrown her apron over her head and was rocking herself to and fro in her grief. But I remarked a small boat fastened to the end of the pier.

"Those two men—they looked like *sous-officiers*—must have come in it, after being too late, I suppose, for the galley. It is incredible that they should have thus broken the regulations from a sense of duty. And it was a stupid thing to do. I could not believe my eyes in the very moment I was stepping into that boat.

"I pulled along the shore slowly. A black cloud hung over the *Iles de Salut*. I heard firing, shouts. Another hunt had begun—the convict-hunt. The oars were too long to pull comfortably. I managed them with difficulty, though the boat herself was light. But when I got round to the other side of the island the squall broke in rain and wind. I was unable to make head against it. I let the boat drift ashore and secured her.

"I knew the spot. There was a tumbledown old hovel standing near the water. Cowering in there I heard through the noises of the wind and the falling downpour some people tearing through the bushes. They came out on the strand. Soldiers perhaps. A flash of lightning threw everything near me into violent relief. Two convicts!" And directly an amazed voice exclaimed. 'It's a miracle!' It was the voice of Simon, otherwise Biscuit.

"And another voice growled, 'What's a miracle?'"

"Why, there's a boat lying here!'

"'You must be mad, Simon! But there is, after all. . . . "A boat.'"

"They seemed awed into complete silence. The other man was Mafile. He spoke again, cautiously.

"'It is fastened up. There must be somebody here.'"

"I spoke to them from within the hovel: 'I am here.'

"They came in then, and soon gave me to understand that the boat was theirs, not mine. 'There are two of us,' said Mafile, 'against you alone.'"

"I got out into the open to keep clear of them for fear of getting a treacherous blow on the head. I could have shot them both where they stood. But I said nothing. I kept down the laughter rising in my throat. I made myself very humble and begged to be allowed to go. They consulted in low tones about my fate, while with my hand on the revolver in the bosom of my blouse I had their lives in my power. I let them live. I meant them to pull that boat. I represented to them with abject humility that I understood the management of a boat, and that, being three to pull, we could get a rest in turns. That decided them at last. It was time. A little more and I would have gone into screaming fits at the drollness of it."

At this point his excitement broke out. He jumped off the bench and gesticulated. The great shadows of his arms darting over roof and walls made the shed appear too small to contain his agitation.

"I deny nothing," he burst out. "I was elated, monsieur. I tasted a sort of felicity. But I kept very quiet. I took my turns at pulling all through the night. We made for the open sea, putting our trust in a passing ship. It was a foolhardy action. I persuaded them to it.

When the sun rose the immensity of water was calm, and the *Iles de Salut* appeared only like dark specks from the top of each swell.

I was steering then. Mafile, who was pulling bow, let out an oath and said, 'We must rest.'

"The time to laugh had come at last. And I took my fill of it, I can tell you. I held my sides and rolled in my seat, they had such startled faces. 'What's got into him, the animal?' cries Mafile.

"And Simon, who was nearest to me, says over his shoulder to him, 'Devil take me if I don't think he's gone mad!'"

"Then I produced the revolver. Aha! In a moment they both got the stoniest eyes you can imagine. Ha, ha! They were frightened.

But they pulled. Oh, yes, they pulled all day, sometimes looking wild and sometimes looking faint. I lost nothing of it because I had to keep my eyes on them all the time, or else—crack!—they would have been on top of me in a second. I rested my revolver hand on my knee all ready and steered with the other.

Their faces began to blister. Sky and sea seemed on fire round us and the sea steamed in the sun. The boat made a sizzling sound as she went through the water. Sometimes Mafile foamed at the mouth and sometimes he groaned. But he pulled. He dared not stop. His eyes became blood-shot all over, and he had bitten his lower lip to pieces. Simon was as hoarse as a crow.

"'Comrade—' he begins.

"'There are no comrades here. I am your *patron*.'"

"*Patron*, then,' he says, 'in the name of humanity let us rest.'

"I let them. There was a little rainwater washing about the bottom of the boat. I permitted them to snatch some of it in the hollow of their palms. But as I gave the command, '*En route*!' I caught them exchanging significant glances. They thought I would have to go to sleep sometime! Aha! But I did not want to go to sleep. I was more awake than ever. It is they who went to sleep as they pulled, tumbling off the thwarts head over heels suddenly, one after another. I let them lie. All the stars were out. It was a quiet world. The sun rose. Another day. *Allez! En route!*

"They pulled badly. Their eyes rolled about and their tongues hung out. In the middle of the forenoon Mafile croaks out: 'Let us make a rush at him, Simon. I would just as soon be shot at once as to die of thirst, hunger, and fatigue at the oar.'

"But while he spoke he pulled; and Simon kept on pulling, too.

"It made me smile. Ah! They loved their life these two, in this evil world of theirs, just as I used to love my life, too, before they spoiled it for me with their phrases. I let them go on to the point of exhaustion, and only then I pointed at the sails of a ship on the horizon.

"Aha! You should have seen them revive and buckle to their work! For I kept them at it to pull right across that ship's path. They were changed. The sort of pity I had felt for them left me. They looked more like themselves every minute. They looked at me with the glances I remembered so well. They were happy. They smiled.

"'Well,' says Simon, 'the energy of that youngster has saved our lives. If he hadn't made us, we could never have pulled so far out into the track of ships. Comrade, I forgive you. I admire you.'"

"And Mafile growls from forward: 'We owe you a famous debt of gratitude, comrade. You are cut out for a chief.'"

"Comrade! Monsieur! Ah, what a good word! And they, such men as these two, had made it accursed. I looked at them. I remembered their lies, their promises, their menaces, and all my days of misery. Why could they not have left me alone after I came out of prison? I looked at them and thought that while they lived I could never be free. Never. Neither I nor others like me with warm hearts and weak heads. For I know I have not a strong head, monsieur. A black rage came upon me—the rage of extreme intoxication—but not against the injustice of society. Oh, no!"

"'I must be free!' I cried, furiously.

"'*Vive la liberte!*'' yells that ruffian Mafile. '*Mort aux bourgeois who send us to Cayenne!* They shall soon know that we are free.'

"The sky, the sea, the whole horizon, seemed to turn red, blood red all round the boat. My temples were beating so loud that I wondered they did not hear. How is it that they did not? How is it they did not understand?"

"I heard Simon ask, 'Have we not pulled far enough out now?'

"'Yes. Far enough,' I said. I was sorry for him; it was the other I hated. He hauled in his oar with a loud sigh, and as he was raising his hand to wipe his forehead with the air of a man who has done his work, I pulled the trigger of my revolver and shot him like this off the knee, right through the heart.

"He tumbled down, with his head hanging over the side of the boat. I did not give him a second glance. The other cried out piercingly. Only one shriek of horror. Then all was still.

"He slipped off the thwart on to his knees and raised his clasped hands before his face in an attitude of supplication. 'Mercy,' he whispered, faintly. 'Mercy for me!—comrade.'"

"'Ah, comrade,' I said, in a low tone. 'Yes, comrade, of course. Well, then, shout *Vive l'anarchie.*'

"He flung up his arms, his face up to the sky and his mouth wide open in a great yell of despair.

'*Vive l'anarchie! Vive—*'

"He collapsed all in a heap, with a bullet through his head.

"I flung them both overboard. I threw away the revolver, too.

"Then I sat down quietly. I was free at last! At last. I did not even look toward the ship; I did not care; indeed, I think I must have gone to sleep, because all of a sudden there were shouts and I found the ship almost on top of me. They hauled me on board and secured the boat astern. They were all blacks, except the captain, who was a mulatto. He alone knew a few words of French. I could not find out where they were going nor who they were. They gave me something to eat every day; but I did not like the way they used to discuss me in their language. Perhaps they were deliberating about throwing me overboard in order to keep possession of the boat. How do I know? As we were passing this island I asked whether it was inhabited. I understood from the mulatto that there was a house on it. A farm, I fancied, they meant. So I asked them to put me ashore on the beach and keep the boat for their trouble.

"This, I imagine, was just what they wanted. The rest you know." After pronouncing these words he lost suddenly all control over himself. He paced to and fro rapidly, till at last he broke into a run; his arms went like a windmill and his ejaculations became very much like raving. The burden of them was that he "denied nothing, nothing!" I could only let him go on, and sat out of his way, repeating, "*Calmez vous, calmez vous*," at intervals, till his agitation exhausted itself.

I must confess, too, that I remained there long after he had crawled under his mosquito-net. He had entreated me not to leave him; so, as one sits up with a nervous child, I sat up with him—in the name of humanity—till he fell asleep.

On the whole, my idea is that he was much more of an anarchist than he confessed to me or to himself; and that, the special features of his case apart, he was very much like many other anarchists.

Warm heart and weak head—that is the word of the riddle; and it is a fact that the bitterest contradictions and the deadliest conflicts of the world are carried on in every individual breast capable of feeling and passion.

From personal inquiry I can vouch that the story of the convict mutiny was in every particular as stated by him.

When I got back to Horta from Cayenne and saw the "Anarchist" again, he did not look well. He was more worn, still more frail, and very livid indeed under the grimy smudges of his calling. Evidently the meat of the company's main herd (in its unconcentrated form) did not agree with him at all.

It was on the pontoon in Horta that we met; and I tried to induce him to leave the launch moored where she was and follow me to Europe there and then. It would have been delightful to think of the excellent manager's surprise and disgust at the poor fellow's escape. But he refused with unconquerable obstinacy.

"Surely you don't mean to live always here!" I cried. He shook his head.

"I shall die here," he said. Then added moodily, "Away from *them*."

Sometimes I think of him lying open-eyed on his horseman's gear in the low shed full of tools and scraps of iron—the anarchist slave of the Marañon estate, waiting with resignation for that sleep which "fled" from him, as he used to say, in such an unaccountable manner.

THE INFORMER

An Ironic Tale

MR. X CAME to me, preceded by a letter of introduction from a good friend of mine in Paris, specifically to see my collection of Chinese bronzes and porcelain.

My friend in Paris is a collector, too. He collects neither porcelain, nor bronzes, nor pictures, nor medals, nor stamps, nor anything that could be profitably dispersed under an auctioneer's hammer. He would reject, with genuine surprise, the name of a collector. Nevertheless, that's what he is by temperament. He collects acquaintances. It is delicate work. He brings to it the patience, the passion, the determination of a true collector of curiosities. His collection does not contain any royal personages. I don't think he considers them sufficiently rare and interesting; but, with that exception, he has met with and talked to everyone worth knowing on any conceivable ground. He observes them, listens to them, penetrates them, measures them, and puts the memory away in the galleries of his mind. He has schemed, plotted, and traveled all over Europe in order to add to his collection of distinguished personal acquaintances.

As he is wealthy, well connected, and unprejudiced, his collection is pretty complete, including objects (or should I say subjects?) whose value is unappreciated by the vulgar, and often unknown to popular fame. Of those specimens my friend is naturally the most proud.

He wrote to me of X: "He is the greatest rebel (*révolté*) of modern times. The world knows him as a revolutionary writer whose savage irony has laid bare the rottenness of the most respectable institutions. He has scalped every venerated head, and has mangled at the stake of his wit every received opinion and every recognized principle of conduct and policy. Who does not remember his flaming red revolutionary pamphlets? Their sudden swarmings used to overwhelm the powers of every Continental police like a plague of crimson gadflies. But this extreme writer has been also the active inspirer of secret societies, the mysterious unknown Number One of desperate conspiracies suspected and unsuspected, matured or baffled. And the world at large has never had an inkling of that fact! This accounts for him going about among us to this day, a veteran of many subterranean campaigns, standing aside now, safe within his reputation of merely the greatest destructive publicist that ever lived."

Thus wrote my friend, adding that Mr. X was an enlightened connoisseur of bronzes and china, and asking me to show him my collection.

X turned up in due course. My treasures are disposed in three large rooms without carpets and curtains. There is no other furniture than the *étagères* and the glass cases whose contents shall be worth a fortune to my heirs. I allow no fires to be lighted, for fear of accidents, and a fire-proof door separates them from the rest of the house.

It was a bitter cold day. We kept on our overcoats and hats. Middle-sized and spare, his eyes alert in a long, Roman-nosed countenance, X walked on his neat little feet, with short steps, and looked at my collection intelligently. I hope I looked at him intelligently, too. A snow-white mustache and imperial made his nut-brown complexion appear darker than it really was. In his fur coat and shiny tall hat that terrible man looked fashionable. I believe he belonged to a noble family, and could have called himself Vicomte X de la Z if he chose. We talked nothing but bronzes and porcelain. He was remarkably appreciative. We parted on cordial terms.

Where he was staying I don't know. I imagine he must have been a lonely man. Anarchists, I suppose, have no families—not, at any rate, as we understand that social relation. Organization into families may answer to a need of human nature, but in the last instance it is based on law, and therefore must be something odious and impossible to an anarchist. But, indeed, I don't understand anarchists. Does a man of that—of that—persuasion still remain an anarchist when alone, quite alone and going to bed, for instance? Does he lay his head on the pillow, pull his bedclothes over him, and go to sleep with the necessity of the *chambardement général*, as the French slang has it, of the general blow-up, always present to his mind? And if so how can he? I am sure that if such a faith (or such a fanaticism) once mastered my thoughts I would never be able to compose myself sufficiently to sleep or eat or perform any of the routine acts of daily life. I would want no wife, no children; I could have no friends, it seems to me; and as to collecting bronzes or china, that, I should say, would be quite out of the question. But I don't know. All I know is that Mr. X took his meals in a very good restaurant which I frequented also.

With his head uncovered, the silver top-knot of his brushed-up hair completed the character of his physiognomy, all bony ridges and sunken hollows, clothed in a perfect impassiveness of expression. His meager brown hands emerging from large white cuffs came and went breaking bread, pouring wine, and so on, with quiet mechanical precision. His head and body above the tablecloth had a rigid immobility. This firebrand, this great agitator, exhibited the least possible amount of warmth and animation. His voice was rasping, cold, and monotonous in a low key. He could not be called a talkative personality; but with his detached calm manner he appeared as ready to keep the conversation going as to drop it at any moment.

And his conversation was by no means commonplace. To me, I own, there was some excitement in talking quietly across a dinner-table with a man whose venomous pen-stabs had sapped the vitality of at least one monarchy. That much was a matter of public knowledge. But I knew more. I knew of him—from my friend—as a certainty what the guardians of social order in Europe had at most only suspected, or dimly guessed at.

He had had what I may call his underground life. And as I sat, evening after evening, facing him at dinner, a curiosity in that direction would naturally arise in my mind. I am a quiet and peaceable product of civilization, and know no passion other than the passion for collecting things which are rare, and must remain exquisite even if approaching to the monstrous. Some Chinese bronzes are monstrously precious. And here (out of my friend's collection), here I had before me a kind of rare monster. It is true that this monster was polished and in a sense even exquisite. His beautiful unruffled manner was that. But then he was not of bronze. He was not even Chinese, which would have enabled one to contemplate him calmly across the gulf of racial difference. He was alive and European; he had the manner of good society, wore a coat and hat like mine, and had pretty near the same taste in cooking. It was too frightful to think of.

One evening he remarked, casually, in the course of conversation, "There's no amendment to be got out of mankind except by terror and violence."

You can imagine the effect of such a phrase out of such a man's mouth upon a person like myself, whose whole scheme of life had been based upon a suave and delicate discrimination of social and artistic values. Just imagine! Upon me, to whom all sorts and forms of violence appeared as unreal as the giants, ogres, and seven-headed hydras whose activities affect, fantastically, the course of legends and fairy-tales!

I seemed suddenly to hear above the festive bustle and clatter of the brilliant restaurant the mutter of a hungry and seditious multitude.

I suppose I am impressionable and imaginative. I had a disturbing vision of darkness, full of lean jaws and wild eyes, among the hundred electric lights of the place. But somehow this vision made me angry, too. The sight of that man, so calm, breaking bits of white bread, exasperated me. And I had the audacity to ask him how it was that the starving proletariat of Europe to whom he had been preaching revolt and violence had not been made indignant by his openly luxurious life. "At all this," I said, pointedly, with a glance round the room and at the bottle of champagne we generally shared between us at dinner.

He remained unmoved.

"Do I feed on their toil and their heart's blood? Am I a speculator or a capitalist? Did I steal my fortune from a starving people? No! They know this very well. And they envy me nothing. The miserable mass of the people is generous to its leaders. What I have acquired has come to me through my writings; not from the millions of pamphlets distributed gratis to the hungry and the oppressed, but from the hundreds of thousands of copies sold to the well-fed bourgeoisie. You know that my writings were at one time the rage, the fashion—the thing to read with wonder and horror, to turn your eyes up at my pathos . . . or else, to laugh in ecstasies at my wit."

"Yes," I admitted. "I remember, of course; and I confess frankly that I could never understand that infatuation."

"Don't you know yet," he said, "that an idle and selfish class loves to see mischief being made, even if it is made at its own expense? Its own life being all a matter of pose and gesture, it is unable to realize the power and the danger of a real movement and of words that have no sham meaning. It is all fun and sentiment. It is sufficient, for instance, to point out the attitude of the old French aristocracy toward the philosophers whose words were preparing the Great Revolution. Even in England, where you have some common-sense, a demagogue has only to shout loud enough and long enough to find some backing in the very class he is shouting at. You, too, like to see mischief being made. The demagogue carries the amateurs of emotion with him. Amateurism in this, that, and the other thing is a delightfully easy way of killing time, and feeding one's own vanity—the silly vanity of being abreast with the ideas of the day after tomorrow. Just as good and otherwise harmless people will join you in ecstasies over your collection without having the slightest notion in what its marvelousness really consists."

I hung my head. It was a crushing illustration of the sad truth he advanced. The world is full of such people. And that instance of the French aristocracy before the Revolution was extremely telling, too. I could not traverse his statement, though its cynicism—always a distasteful trait—took off much of its value to my mind. However, I admit I was impressed. I felt the need to say something which would not be in the nature of assent and yet would not invite discussion.

"You don't mean to say," I observed, airily, "that extreme revolutionists have ever been actively assisted by the infatuation of such people?"

"I did not mean exactly that by what I said just now. I generalized. But since you ask me, I may tell you that such help has been given to revolutionary activities, more or less consciously, in various countries. And even in this country."

"Impossible!" I protested with firmness. "We don't play with fire to that extent."

"And yet you can better afford it than others, perhaps. But let me observe that most women, if not always ready to play with fire, are generally eager to play with a loose spark or so."

"Is this a joke?" I asked, smiling.

"If it is, I am not aware of it," he said, woodenly. "I was thinking of an instance. Oh! mild enough in a way . . ."

I became all expectation at this. I had tried many times to approach him on his underground side, so to speak. The very word had been pronounced between us. But he had always met me with his impenetrable calm.

"And at the same time," Mr. X continued, "it will give you a notion of the difficulties that may arise in what you are pleased to call underground work. It is sometimes difficult to deal with them. Of course there is no hierarchy among the affiliated. No rigid system."

My surprise was great, but short-lived. Clearly, among extreme anarchists there could be no hierarchy; nothing in the nature of a law of precedence. The idea of anarchy ruling among anarchists was comforting, too. It could not possibly make for efficiency.

Mr. X startled me by asking, abruptly, "You know Hermione Street?"

I nodded doubtful assent. Hermione Street has been, within the last three years, improved out of any man's knowledge. The name exists still, but not one brick or stone of the old Hermione Street is left now.

It was the old street he meant, for he said: "There was a row of two-storied brick houses on the left, with their backs against the wing of a great public building—you remember. Would it surprise you very much to hear that one of these houses was for a time the center of anarchist propaganda and of what you would call underground action?"

"Not at all," I declared. Hermione Street had never been particularly respectable, as I remembered it.

"The house was the property of a distinguished government official," he added, sipping his champagne.

"Oh, indeed!" I said, this time not believing a word of it.

"Of course he was not living there," Mr. X continued. "But from ten till four he sat next door to it, the dear man, in his well-appointed private room in the wing of the public building I've mentioned. To be strictly accurate, I must explain that the house in Hermione Street did not really belong to him. It belonged to his grown-up children—a daughter and a son. The girl, a fine figure, was by no means vulgarly pretty. To more personal charm than mere youth could account for, she added the seductive appearance of enthusiasm, of independence, of courageous thought. I suppose she put on these appearances as she put on her picturesque dresses and for the same reason: to assert her individuality at any cost. You know, women would go to any length almost for such a purpose. She went to a great length. She had acquired all the appropriate gestures of revolutionary convictions—the gestures of pity, of anger, of indignation against the anti-humanitarian vices of the social class to which she belonged herself. All this sat on her striking personality as well as her slightly original costumes. Very slightly original; just enough to mark a protest against the philistinism of the overfed taskmasters of the poor. Just enough, and no more. It would not have done to go too far in that direction—you understand. But she was of age, and nothing stood in the way of her offering her house to the revolutionary workers."

"You don't mean it!" I cried.

"I assure you," he affirmed, "that she made that very practical gesture. How else could they have got hold of it? The cause is not rich. And, moreover, there would have been difficulties with any ordinary house-agent, who would have wanted references and so on. The group she came in contact with while exploring the poor quarters of the town (you know the gesture of charity and personal service which was so fashionable some years ago) accepted with gratitude. The first advantage was that Hermione Street is, as you know, well away from the suspect part of the town, specially watched by the police.

"The ground floor consisted of a little Italian restaurant, of the fly-blown sort. There was no difficulty in buying the proprietor out. A woman and a man belonging to the group took it on. The man had been a cook. The comrades could get their meals there, unnoticed among the other customers. This was another advantage. The first floor was occupied by a shabby Variety Artists' Agency—an agency for performers in inferior music-halls, you know. A fellow called Bomm, I remember. He was not disturbed. It was rather favorable than otherwise to have a lot of foreign-looking people, jugglers, acrobats, singers of both sexes, and so on, going in and out all day long. The police paid no attention to new faces, you see. The top floor happened, most conveniently, to stand empty then."

X interrupted himself to attack impassively, with measured movements, a *bombe glacée* which the waiter had just set down on the table. He swallowed carefully a few spoonfuls of the iced sweet, and asked me, "Did you ever hear of Stone's Dried Soup?"

"Hear of what?"

"It was," X pursued, evenly, "a comestible article once rather prominently advertised in the dailies, but which never, somehow, gained the favor of the public. The enterprise fizzled out, as you say here. Parcels of their stock could be picked up at auctions at considerably less than a penny a pound. The group bought some of it, and an agency for Stone's Dried Soup was started on the top floor. A perfectly respectable business. The stuff, a yellow powder of extremely unappetizing aspect, was put up in large square tins, of which six went to a case. If anybody ever came to give an order, it was, of course, executed. But the advantage of the powder was this, that things could be concealed in it very conveniently. Now and then a special case got put on a van and sent off to be exported abroad under the very nose of the policeman on duty at the corner. You understand?"

"I think I do," I said, with an expressive nod at the remnants of the *bombe* melting slowly in the dish.

"Exactly. But the cases were useful in another way, too. In the basement, or in the cellar at the back, rather, two printing-presses were established. A lot of revolutionary literature of the most inflammatory kind was got away from the house in Stone's Dried Soup cases. The brother of our anarchist young lady found some occupation there. He wrote articles, helped to set up type and pull off the sheets, and generally assisted the man in charge, a very able young fellow called Sevrin.

"The guiding spirit of that group was a fanatic of social revolution. He is dead now. He was an engraver and etcher of genius. You must have seen his work. It is much sought after by certain amateurs now. He began by being revolutionary in his art, and ended by becoming a revolutionist, after his wife and child had died in want and misery. He used to say that the bourgeoisie, the smug, overfed lot, had killed them. That was his real belief. He still worked at his art and led a double life. He was tall, gaunt, and swarthy, with a long, brown beard and deep-set eyes. You must have seen him. His name was Horne."

At this I was really startled. Of course years ago I used to meet Horne about. He looked like a powerful, rough gypsy, in an old top hat, with a red muffler round his throat and buttoned up in a long, shabby overcoat. He talked of his art with exaltation, and gave one the impression of being strung up to the verge of insanity. A small group of connoisseurs appreciated his work. Who would have thought that this man. . . . Amazing! And yet it was not, after all, so difficult to believe.

"As you see," X went on, "this group was in a position to pursue its work of propaganda, and the other kind of work, too, under very advantageous conditions. They were all resolute, experienced men of a superior stamp. And yet we became struck at length by the fact that plans prepared in Hermione Street almost invariably failed."

"Who were 'we'?" I asked, pointedly.

"Some of us in Brussels—at the center," he said, hastily. "Whatever vigorous action originated in Hermione Street seemed doomed to failure. Something always happened to baffle the best planned manifestations in every part of Europe. It was a time of general activity. You must not imagine that all our failures are of a loud sort, with arrests and trials. That is not so. Often the police work quietly, almost secretly, defeating our combinations by clever counter-plotting. No arrests, no noise, no alarming of the public mind and inflaming the passions. It is a wise procedure. But at that time the police were too uniformly successful from the Mediterranean to the Baltic. It was annoying and began to look dangerous. At last we came to the conclusion that there must be some untrustworthy elements among the London groups. And I came over to see what could be done quietly.

"My first step was to call upon our young Lady Amateur of anarchism at her private house. She received me in a flattering way. I judged that she knew nothing of the chemical and other operations going on at the top of the house in Hermione Street. The printing of anarchist literature was the only 'activity' she seemed to be aware of there. She was displaying very strikingly the usual signs of severe enthusiasm, and had already written many sentimental articles with ferocious conclusions. I could see she was enjoying herself hugely, with all the gestures and grimaces of deadly earnestness. They suited her big-eyed, broad-browed face and the good carriage of her shapely head, crowned by a magnificent lot of brown hair done in an unusual and becoming style. Her brother was in the room, too, a serious youth, with arched eyebrows and wearing a red necktie, who struck me as being absolutely in the dark about everything in the world, including himself. By and by a tall young man came in. He was clean-shaved with a strong bluish jaw and something of the air of a taciturn actor or of a fanatical priest: the type with thick black eyebrows—you know. But he was very presentable indeed. He shook hands at once vigorously with each of us. The young lady came up to me and murmured sweetly, 'Comrade Sevrin.'

"I had never seen him before. He had little to say to us, but sat down by the side of the girl, and they fell at once into earnest conversation. She leaned forward in her deep armchair, and took her nicely rounded chin in her beautiful white hand. He looked attentively into her eyes. It was the attitude of love-making, serious, intense, as if on the brink of the grave. I suppose she felt it necessary to round and complete her assumption of advanced ideas, of revolutionary lawlessness, by making believe to be in love with an anarchist. And this one, I repeat, was extremely presentable, notwithstanding his fanatical black-browed aspect. After a few stolen glances in their direction, I had no doubt that he was in earnest. As to the lady, her gestures were unapproachable, better than the very thing itself in the blended suggestion of dignity, sweetness, condescension, fascination, surrender, and reserve. She interpreted her conception of what that precise sort of love-making should be with consummate art. And so far, she, too, no doubt, was in earnest. Gestures—but so perfect!

"After I had been left alone with our Lady Amateur I informed her guardedly of the object of my visit. I hinted at our suspicions. I wanted to hear what she would have to say, and half expected some perhaps unconscious revelation. All she said was, 'That's serious,' looking delightfully concerned and grave. But there was a sparkle in her eyes which meant plainly, 'How exciting!' After all, she knew little of anything except of words. Still, she undertook to put me in communication with Horne, who was not easy to find unless in Hermione Street, where I did not wish to show myself just then.

"I met Horne. This was another kind of a fanatic altogether. I exposed to him the conclusion we in Brussels had arrived at, and pointed out the significant series of failures. To this he answered with irrelevant exaltation:

"'I have something in hand that shall strike terror into the heart of these gorged brutes.'

"And then I learned that, by excavating in one of the cellars of the house, he and some companions had made their way into the vaults under the great public building I have mentioned before. The blowing up of a whole wing was a certainty as soon as the materials were ready.

"I was not so appalled at the stupidity of that move as I might have been had not the usefulness of our center in Hermione Street become already very problematical. In fact, in my opinion it was much more of a police trap by this time than anything else.

"What was necessary now was to discover what, or rather who, was wrong, and I managed at last to get that idea into Horne's head. He glared, perplexed, his nostrils working as if he were sniffing treachery in the air.

"And here comes a piece of work which will no doubt strike you as a sort of theatrical expedient. And yet what else could have been done? The problem was to find out the untrustworthy member of the group. But no suspicion could be fastened on one more than another. To set a watch upon them all was not very practicable. Besides, that proceeding often fails. In any case, it takes time, and the danger was pressing. I felt certain that the premises in Hermione Street would be ultimately raided, though the police had evidently such confidence in the informer that the house, for the time being, was not even watched. Horne was positive on that point. Under the circumstances it was an unfavorable symptom. Something had to be done quickly.

"I decided to organize a raid myself upon the group. Do you understand? A raid of other trusty comrades personating the police. A conspiracy within a conspiracy. You see the object of it, of course. When apparently about to be arrested I hoped the informer would betray himself in some way or other; either by some unguarded act or simply by his unconcerned demeanor, for instance. Of coarse there was the risk of complete failure and the no lesser risk of some fatal accident in the course of resistance, perhaps, or in the efforts at escape. For, as you will easily see, the Hermione Street group had to be actually and completely taken unawares, as I was sure they would be by the real police before very long. The informer was among them, and Horne alone could be let into the secret of my plan.

"I will not enter into the detail of my preparations. It was not very easy to arrange, but it was done very well, with a really convincing effect. The sham police invaded the restaurant, whose shutters were immediately put up. The surprise was perfect. Most of the Hermione Street party were found in the second cellar, enlarging the hole communicating with the vaults of the great public building. At the first alarm, several comrades bolted through impulsively into the aforesaid vault, where, of course, had this been a genuine raid, they would have been hopelessly trapped. We did not bother about them for the moment. They were harmless enough. The top floor caused considerable anxiety to Horne and myself. There, surrounded by tins of Stone's Dried Soup, a comrade, nicknamed the Professor (he was an ex-science student) was engaged in perfecting some new detonators. He was an abstracted, self-confident, sallow little man, armed with large round spectacles, and we were afraid that under a mistaken impression he would blow himself up and wreck the house about our ears. I rushed upstairs and found him already at the door, on the alert, listening, as he said, to 'suspicious noises down below.' Before I had quite finished explaining to him what was going on he shrugged his shoulders disdainfully and turned away to his balances and test-tubes. His was the true spirit of an extreme revolutionist. Explosives were his faith, his hope, his weapon, and his shield. He perished a couple of years afterwards in a secret laboratory through the premature explosion of one of his improved detonators.

"Hurrying down again, I found an impressive scene in the gloom of the big cellar. The man who personated the inspector (he was no stranger to the part) was speaking harshly, and giving bogus orders to his bogus subordinates for the removal of his prisoners. Evidently nothing enlightening had happened so far. Horne, saturnine and swarthy, waited with folded arms, and his patient, moody expectation had an air of stoicism well in keeping with the situation. I detected in the shadows one of the Hermione Street group surreptitiously chewing up and swallowing a small piece of paper. Some compromising scrap, I suppose; perhaps just a note of a few names and addresses. He was a true and faithful 'companion.' But the fund of secret malice which lurks at the bottom of our sympathies caused me to feel amused at that perfectly uncalled-for performance.

"In every other respect the risky experiment, the theatrical coup, if you like to call it so, seemed to have failed. The deception could not be kept up much longer; the explanation would bring about a very embarrassing and even grave situation. The man who had eaten the paper would be furious. The fellows who had bolted away would be angry, too.

"To add to my vexation, the door communicating with the other cellar, where the printing-presses were, flew open, and our young lady revolutionist appeared, a black silhouette in a close-fitting dress and a large hat, with the blaze of gas flaring in there at her back. Over her shoulder I perceived the arched eyebrows and the red necktie of her brother.

"The last people in the world I wanted to see then! They had gone that evening to some amateur concert for the delectation of the poor people, you know; but she had insisted on leaving early, on purpose to call in Hermione Street on the way home, under the pretext of having some work to do. Her usual task was to correct the proofs of the Italian and French editions of the *Alarm Bell* and the *Firebrand*." . . .

"Heavens!" I murmured. I had been shown once a few copies of these publications. Nothing, in my opinion, could have been less fit for the eyes of a young lady. They were the most advanced things of the sort; advanced, I mean, beyond all bounds of reason and decency. One of them preached the dissolution of all social and domestic ties; the other advocated systematic murder. To think of a young girl calmly tracking printers' errors all along the sort of abominable sentences I remembered was intolerable to my sentiment of womanhood. Mr. X, after giving me a glance, pursued steadily.

"I think, however, that she came mostly to exercise her fascinations upon Sevrin, and to receive his homage in her queenly and condescending way. She was aware of both—her power and his homage—and enjoyed them with, I dare say, complete innocence. We have no ground in expediency or morals to quarrel with her on that account. Charm in woman and exceptional intelligence in man are a law unto themselves. Is it not so?"

I refrained from expressing my abhorrence of that licentious doctrine because of my curiosity.

"But what happened then?" I hastened to ask.

X went on crumbling slowly a small piece of bread with a careless left hand.

"What happened, in effect," he confessed, "is that she saved the situation."

"She gave you an opportunity to end your rather sinister farce," I suggested.

"Yes," he said, preserving his impassive bearing. "The farce was bound to end soon. And it ended in a very few minutes. And it ended well. Had she not come in, it might have ended badly. Her brother, of course, did not count. They had slipped into the house quietly some time before. The printing-cellar had an entrance of its own. Not finding anyone there, she sat down to her proofs, expecting Sevrin to return to his work at any moment. He did not do so. She grew impatient, heard through the door the sounds of a disturbance in the other cellar and naturally came in to see what was the matter.

"Sevrin had been with us. At first he had seemed to me the most amazed of the whole raided lot. He appeared for an instant as if paralyzed with astonishment. He stood rooted to the spot. He never moved a limb. A solitary gas-jet flared near his head; all the other lights had been put out at the first alarm. And presently, from my dark corner, I observed on his shaven actor's face an expression of puzzled, vexed watchfulness. He knitted his heavy eyebrows. The corners of his mouth dropped scornfully. He was angry. Most likely he had seen through the game, and I regretted I had not taken him from the first into my complete confidence.

"But with the appearance of the girl he became obviously alarmed. It was plain. I could see it grow. The change of his expression was swift and startling. And I did not know why. The reason never occurred to me. I was merely astonished at the extreme alteration of the man's face. Of course he had not been aware of her presence in the other cellar; but that did not explain the shock her advent had given him. For a moment he seemed to have been reduced to imbecility. He opened his mouth as if to shout, or perhaps only to gasp. At any rate, it was somebody else who shouted. This somebody else was the heroic comrade whom I had detected swallowing a piece of paper. With laudable presence of mind he let out a warning yell.

"'It's the police! Back! Back! Run back, and bolt the door behind you.'

"It was an excellent hint; but instead of retreating the girl continued to advance, followed by her long-faced brother in his knickerbocker suit, in which he had been singing comic songs for the entertainment of a joyless proletariat. She advanced not as if she had failed to understand—the word 'police' has an unmistakable sound—but rather as if she could not help herself. She did not advance with the free gait and expanding presence of a distinguished amateur anarchist among poor, struggling professionals, but with slightly raised shoulders, and her elbows pressed close to her body, as if trying to shrink within herself. Her eyes were fixed immovably upon Sevrin. Sevrin the man, I fancy; not Sevrin the anarchist. But she advanced. And that was natural. For all their assumption of independence, girls of that class are used to the feeling of being specially protected, as, in fact, they are. This feeling accounts for nine-tenths of their audacious gestures. Her face had gone completely colorless. Ghastly. Fancy having it brought home to her so brutally that she was the sort of person who must run away from the police! I believe she was pale with indignation, mostly, though there was, of course, also the concern for her intact personality, a vague dread of some sort of rudeness. And, naturally, she turned to a man, to the man on whom she had a claim of fascination and homage—the man who could not conceivably fail her at any juncture."

"But," I cried, amazed at this analysis, "if it had been serious, real, I mean—as she thought it was—what could she expect him to do for her?"

X never moved a muscle of his face.

"Goodness knows. I imagine that this charming, generous, and independent creature had never known in her life a single genuine thought; I mean a single thought detached from small human vanities, or whose source was not in some conventional perception. All I know is that after advancing a few steps she extended her hand toward the motionless Sevrin. And that at least was no gesture. It was a natural movement. As to what she expected him to do, who can tell? The impossible. But whatever she expected, it could not have come up, I am safe to say, to what he had made up his mind to do, even before that entreating hand had appealed to him so directly. It had not been necessary. From the moment he had seen her enter that cellar, he had made up his mind to sacrifice his future usefulness, to throw off the impenetrable, solidly fastened mask it had been his pride to wear—"

"What do you mean?" I interrupted, puzzled. "Was it Sevrin, then, who was—"

"He was. The most persistent, the most dangerous, the craftiest, the most systematic of informers. A genius among betrayers. Fortunately for us, he was unique. The man was a fanatic, I have told you. Fortunately, again, for us, he had fallen in love with the accomplished and innocent gestures of that girl. An actor in desperate earnest himself, he must have believed in the absolute value of conventional signs. As to the grossness of the trap into which he fell, the explanation must be that two sentiments of such absorbing magnitude cannot exist simultaneously in one heart. The danger of that other and unconscious comedian robbed him of his vision, of his perspicacity, of his judgment. Indeed, it did at first rob him of his self-possession. But he regained that through the necessity—as it appeared to him imperiously—to do something at once. To do what? Why, to get her out of the house as quickly as possible. He was desperately anxious to do that. I have told you he was terrified. It could not be about himself. He had been surprised and annoyed at a move quite unforeseen and premature. I may even say he had been furious. He was accustomed to arrange the last scene of his betrayals with a deep, subtle art which left his revolutionist reputation untouched. But it seems clear to me that at the same time he had resolved to make the best of it, to keep his mask resolutely on. It was only with the discovery of her being in the house that everything—the forced calm, the restraint of his fanaticism, the mask—all came off together in a kind of panic. Why panic, do you ask? The answer is very simple. He remembered—or, I dare say, he had never forgotten—the Professor alone at the top of the house, pursuing his researches, surrounded by tins upon tins of Stone's Dried Soup. There was enough in some few of them to bury us all where we stood under a heap of bricks. Sevrin, of course, was aware of that. And we must believe, also, that he knew the exact character of the man. He had gauged so many such characters! Or perhaps he only gave the Professor credit for what he himself was capable of. But, in any case, the effect was produced. And suddenly he raised his voice in authority.

"'Get the lady away at once.'

"It turned out that he was as hoarse as a crow; result, no doubt, of the intense emotion. It passed off in a moment. But these fateful words issued forth from his contracted throat in a discordant, ridiculous croak. They required no answer. The thing was done. However, the man personating the inspector judged it expedient to say roughly:

"'She shall go soon enough, together with the rest of you.'

"These were the last words belonging to the comedy part of this affair.

"Oblivious of everything and everybody, Sevrin strode toward him and seized the lapels of his coat. Under his thin bluish cheeks one could see his jaws working with passion.

"'You have men posted outside. Get the lady taken home at once. Do you hear? Now. Before you try to get hold of the man upstairs.'

"'Oh! There is a man upstairs,' scoffed the other, openly. 'Well, he shall be brought down in time to see the end of this.'

"But Sevrin, beside himself, took no heed of the tone.

"'Who's the imbecile meddler who sent you blundering here? Didn't you understand your instructions? Don't you know anything? It's incredible. Here—'

"He dropped the lapels of the coat and, plunging his hand into his breast, jerked feverishly at something under his shirt. At last he produced a small square pocket of soft leather, which must have been hanging like a scapulary from his neck by the tape whose broken ends dangled from his fist.

"'Look inside,' he spluttered, flinging it in the other's face. And instantly he turned round toward the girl. She stood just behind him, perfectly still and silent. Her set, white face gave an illusion of placidity. Only her staring eyes seemed bigger and darker.

"He spoke rapidly, with nervous assurance. I heard him distinctly promise her to make everything as clear as daylight presently. But that was all I caught. He stood close to her, never attempting to touch her even with the tip of his little finger—and she stared at him stupidly. For a moment, however, her eyelids descended slowly, pathetically, and then, with the long black eyelashes lying on her white cheeks, she looked ready to fall down in a swoon. But she never even swayed where she stood. He urged her loudly to follow him at once, and walked toward the door at the bottom of the cellar stairs without looking behind him. And, as a matter of fact, she did move after him a pace or two. But, of course, he was not allowed to reach the door. There were angry exclamations, a short, fierce scuffle. Flung away violently, he came flying backwards upon her, and fell. She threw out her arms in a gesture of dismay and stepped aside, just clear of his head, which struck the ground heavily near her shoe.

"He grunted with the shock. By the time he had picked himself up, slowly, dazedly, he was awake to the reality of things. The man into whose hands he had thrust the leather case had extracted therefrom a narrow strip of bluish paper. He held it up above his head, and, as after the scuffle an expectant uneasy stillness reigned once more, he threw it down disdainfully with the words, 'I think, comrades, that this proof was hardly necessary.'

"Quick as thought, the girl stooped after the fluttering slip. Holding it spread out in both hands, she looked at it; then, without raising her eyes, opened her fingers slowly and let it fall.

"I examined that curious document afterwards. It was signed by a very high personage, and stamped and countersigned by other high officials in various countries of Europe. In his trade—or shall I say, in his mission?—that sort of talisman might have been necessary, no doubt. Even to the police itself—all but the heads—he had been known only as Sevrin the noted anarchist.

"He hung his head, biting his lower lip. A change had come over him, a sort of thoughtful, absorbed calmness. Nevertheless, he panted. His sides worked visibly, and his nostrils expanded and collapsed in weird contrast with his somber aspect of a fanatical monk in a meditative attitude, but with something, too, in his face of an actor intent upon the terrible exigencies of his part. Before him Horne declaimed, haggard and bearded, like an inspired denunciatory prophet from a wilderness. Two fanatics. They were made to understand each other. Does this surprise you? I suppose you think that such people would be foaming at the mouth and snarling at each other?"

I protested hastily that I was not surprised in the least; that I thought nothing of the kind; that anarchists in general were simply inconceivable to me mentally, morally, logically, sentimentally, and even physically. X received this declaration with his usual woodenness and went on.

"Horne had burst out into eloquence. While pouring out scornful invective, he let tears escape from his eyes and roll down his black beard unheeded. Sevrin panted quicker and quicker. When he opened his mouth to speak, everyone hung on his words.

"'Don't be a fool, Horne,' he began. 'You know very well that I have done this for none of the reasons you are throwing at me.' And in a moment he became outwardly as steady as a rock under the other's lurid stare. 'I have been thwarting, deceiving, and betraying you—from conviction.'

"He turned his back on Horne, and addressing the girl, repeated the words: 'From conviction.'

"It's extraordinary how cold she looked. I suppose she could not think of any appropriate gesture. There can have been few precedents indeed for such a situation.

"'Clear as daylight,' he added. 'Do you understand what that means? From conviction.'

"And still she did not stir. She did not know what to do. But the luckless wretch was about to give her the opportunity for a beautiful and correct gesture.

"'I have felt in me the power to make you share this conviction,' he protested, ardently. He had forgotten himself; he made a step toward her—perhaps he stumbled. To me he seemed to be stooping low as if to touch the hem of her garment. And then the appropriate gesture came. She snatched her skirt away from his polluting contact and averted her head with an upward tilt. It was magnificently done, this gesture of conventionally unstained honor, of an unblemished high-minded amateur.

"Nothing could have been better. And he seemed to think so, too, for once more he turned away. But this time he faced no one. He was again panting frightfully, while he fumbled hurriedly in his waistcoat pocket, and then raised his hand to his lips. There was something furtive in this movement, but directly afterwards his bearing changed. His labored breathing gave him a resemblance to a man who had just run a desperate race; but a curious air of detachment, of sudden and profound indifference, replaced the strain of the striving effort. The race was over. I did not want to see what would happen next. I was only too well aware. I tucked the young lady's arm under mine without a word, and made my way with her to the stairs.

"Her brother walked behind us. Halfway up the short flight she seemed unable to lift her feet high enough for the steps, and we had to pull and push to get her to the top. In the passage she dragged herself along, hanging on my arm, helplessly bent like an old woman. We issued into an empty street through a half-open door, staggering like besotted revelers. At the corner we stopped a four-wheeler, and the ancient driver looked round from his box with morose scorn at our efforts to get her in. Twice during the drive I felt her collapse on my shoulder in a half faint. Facing us, the youth in knickerbockers remained as mute as a fish, and, till he jumped out with the latch-key, sat more still than I would have believed it possible.

"At the door of their drawing room she left my arm and walked in first, catching at the chairs and tables. She unpinned her hat, then, exhausted with the effort, her cloak still hanging from her shoulders, flung herself into a deep armchair, sideways, her face half buried in a cushion. The good brother appeared silently before her with a glass of water. She motioned it away. He drank it himself and walked off to a distant corner—behind the grand piano, somewhere. All was still in this room where I had seen, for the first time, Sevrin, the anti-anarchist, captivated and spellbound by the consummate and hereditary grimaces that in a certain sphere of life take the place of feelings with an excellent effect. I suppose her thoughts were busy with the same memory. Her shoulders shook violently. A pure attack of nerves. When it quieted down she affected firmness, 'What is done to a man of that sort? What will they do to him?'

"'Nothing. They can do nothing to him,' I assured her, with perfect truth. I was pretty certain he had died in less than twenty minutes from the moment his hand had gone to his lips. For if his fanatical anti-anarchism went even as far as carrying poison in his pocket, only to rob his adversaries of legitimate vengeance, I knew he would take care to provide something that would not fail him when required.

"She drew an angry breath. There were red spots on her cheeks and a feverish brilliance in her eyes.

"'Has ever anyone been exposed to such a terrible experience? To think that he had held my hand! That man!' Her face twitched, she gulped down a pathetic sob. 'If I ever felt sure of anything, it was of Sevrin's high-minded motives.'

"Then she began to weep quietly, which was good for her. Then through her flood of tears, half resentful, 'What was it he said to me?—"From conviction!" It seemed a vile mockery. What could he mean by it?'

"'That, my dear young lady,' I said, gently, 'is more than I or anybody else can ever explain to you.'"

Mr. X flicked a crumb off the front of his coat.

"And that was strictly true as to her. Though Horne, for instance, understood very well; and so did I, especially after we had been to Sevrin's lodging in a dismal back street of an intensely respectable quarter. Horne was known there as a friend, and we had no difficulty in being admitted, the slatternly maid merely remarking, as she let us in, that 'Mr Sevrin had not been home that night.' We forced open a couple of drawers in the way of duty, and found a little useful information. The most interesting part was his diary; for this man, engaged in such deadly work, had the weakness to keep a record of the most damnatory kind. There were his acts and also his thoughts laid bare to us. But the dead don't mind that. They don't mind anything.

"'From conviction.' Yes. A vague but ardent humanitarianism had urged him in his first youth into the bitterest extremity of negation and revolt. Afterwards his optimism flinched. He doubted and became lost. You have heard of converted atheists. These turn often into dangerous fanatics, but the soul remains the same. After he had got acquainted with the girl, there are to be met in that diary of his very queer politico-amorous rhapsodies. He took her sovereign grimaces with deadly seriousness. He longed to convert her. But all this cannot interest you. For the rest, I don't know if you remember—it is a good many years ago now—the journalistic sensation of the 'Hermione Street Mystery'; the finding of a man's body in the cellar of an empty house; the inquest; some arrests; many surmises—then silence—the usual end for many obscure martyrs and confessors. The fact is, he was not enough of an optimist. You must be a savage, tyrannical, pitiless, thick-and-thin optimist, like Horne, for instance, to make a good social rebel of the extreme type.

"He rose from the table. A waiter hurried up with his overcoat; another held his hat in readiness.

"But what became of the young lady?" I asked.

"Do you really want to know?" he said, buttoning himself in his fur coat carefully. "I confess to the small malice of sending her Sevrin's diary. She went into retirement; then she went to Florence; then she went into retreat in a convent. I can't tell where she will go next. What does it matter? Gestures! Gestures! Mere gestures of her class."

"He fitted on his glossy high hat with extreme precision, and casting a rapid glance round the room, full of well-dressed people, innocently dining, muttered between his teeth:

"And nothing else! That is why their kind is fated to perish."

I never met Mr. X again after that evening. I took to dining at my club. On my next visit to Paris I found my friend all impatience to hear of the effect produced on me by this rare item of his collection. I told him all the story, and he beamed on me with the pride of his distinguished specimen.

"Isn't X well worth knowing?" he bubbled over in great delight. "He's unique, amazing, absolutely terrific."

His enthusiasm grated upon my finer feelings. I told him curtly that the man's cynicism was simply abominable.

"Oh, abominable! abominable!" assented my friend, effusively. "And then, you know, he likes to have his little joke sometimes," he added in a confidential tone.

I fail to understand the connection of this last remark. I have been utterly unable to discover where in all this the joke comes in.

IL CONDE

A Pathetic Tale

Vedi Napoli e poi mori.

The first time we got into conversation was in the National Museum in Naples, in the rooms on the ground floor containing the famous collection of bronzes from Herculaneum and Pompeii: that marvelous legacy of antique art whose delicate perfection has been preserved for us by the catastrophic fury of a volcano.

He addressed me first, over the celebrated Resting Hermes which we had been looking at side by side. He said the right things about that wholly admirable piece. Nothing profound. His taste was natural rather than cultivated. He had obviously seen many fine things in his life and appreciated them: but he had no jargon of a dilettante or the connoisseur. A hateful tribe. He spoke like a fairly intelligent man of the world, a perfectly unaffected gentleman.

We had known each other by sight for some few days past. Staying in the same hotel—good, but not extravagantly up to date—I had noticed him in the vestibule going in and out. I judged he was an old and valued client. The bow of the hotel-keeper was cordial in its deference, and he acknowledged it with familiar courtesy. For the servants he was Il Conde. There was some squabble over a man's parasol—yellow silk with white lining sort of thing—the waiters had discovered abandoned outside the dining room door. Our gold-laced door-keeper recognized it and I heard him directing one of the lift boys to run after *Il Conde* with it. Perhaps he was the only Count staying in the hotel, or perhaps he had the distinction of being *the* Count *par excellence*, conferred upon him because of his tried fidelity to the house.

Having conversed at the Museo—(and by the by he had expressed his dislike of the busts and statues of Roman emperors in the gallery of marbles: their faces were too vigorous, too pronounced for him)—

having conversed already in the morning I did not think I was intruding when in the evening, finding the dining room very full, I proposed to share his little table. Judging by the quiet urbanity of his consent he did not think so either. His smile was very attractive.

He dined in an evening waistcoat and a "smoking" (he called it so) with a black tie. All this of very good cut, not new—just as these things should be. He was, morning or evening, very correct in his dress. I have no doubt that his whole existence had been correct, well ordered and conventional, undisturbed by startling events. His white hair brushed upwards off a lofty forehead gave him the air of an idealist, of an imaginative man. His white mustache, heavy but carefully trimmed and arranged, was not unpleasantly tinted a golden yellow in the middle. The faint scent of some very good perfume, and of good cigars (that last an odor quite remarkable to come upon in Italy) reached me across the table. It was in his eyes that his age showed most. They were a little weary with creased eyelids. He must have been sixty or a couple of years more. And he was communicative. I would not go so far as to call it garrulous—but distinctly communicative.

He had tried various climates, of Abbazia, of the Riviera, of other places, too, he told me, but the only one which suited him was the climate of the Gulf of Naples. The ancient Romans, who, he pointed out to me, were men expert in the art of living, knew very well what they were doing when they built their villas on these shores, in Baiae, in Vico, in Capri. They came down to this seaside in search of health, bringing with them their trains of mimes and flute-players to amuse their leisure. He thought it extremely probable that the Romans of the higher classes were specially predisposed to painful rheumatic affections.

This was the only personal opinion I heard him express. It was based on no special erudition. He knew no more of the Romans than an average informed man of the world is expected to know. He argued from personal experience. He had suffered himself from a painful and dangerous rheumatic affection till he found relief in this particular spot of Southern Europe.

This was three years ago, and ever since he had taken up his quarters on the shores of the gulf, either in one of the hotels in Sorrento or hiring a small villa in Capri. He had a piano, a few books: picked up transient acquaintances of a day, week, or month in the stream of travelers from all Europe. One can imagine him going out for his walks in the streets and lanes, becoming known to beggars, shopkeepers, children, country people; talking amiably over the walls to the *contadini*—and coming back to his rooms or his villa to sit before the piano, with his white hair brushed up and his thick orderly mustache, "to make a little music for myself." And, of course, for a change there was Naples near by—life, movement, animation, opera. A little amusement, as he said, is necessary for health. Mimes and flute-players, in fact. Only unlike the magnates of ancient Rome, he had no affairs of the city to call him away from these moderate delights. He had no affairs at all. Probably he had never had any grave affairs to attend to in his life. It was a kindly existence, with its joys and sorrows regulated by the course of Nature—marriages, births, deaths—ruled by the prescribed usages of good society and protected by the State.

He was a widower; but in the months of July and August he ventured to cross the Alps for six weeks on a visit to his married daughter. He told me her name. It was that of a very aristocratic family. She had a castle—in Bohemia, I think. This is as near as I ever came to ascertaining his nationality. His own name, strangely enough, he never mentioned. Perhaps he thought I had seen it on the published list. Truth to say, I never looked. At any rate, he was a good European—he spoke four languages to my certain knowledge—and a man of fortune. Not of great fortune evidently and appropriately. I imagine that to be extremely rich would have appeared to him improper, *outré*—too blatant altogether. And obviously, too, the fortune was not of his making. The making of a fortune cannot be achieved without some roughness. It is a matter of temperament. His nature was too kindly for strife. In the course of conversation he mentioned his estate quite by the way, in reference to that painful and alarming rheumatic affection. One year, staying incautiously beyond the Alps as late as the middle of September, he had been laid up for three months in that lonely country house with no one but his valet and the caretaking couple to attend to him. Because, as he expressed it, he "kept no establishment there." He had only gone for a couple of days to confer with his land agent. He promised himself never to be so imprudent in the future. The first weeks of September would find him on the shores of his beloved gulf.

Sometimes in traveling one comes upon such lonely men, whose only business is to wait for the unavoidable. Deaths and marriages have made a solitude round them, and one really cannot blame their endeavors to make the waiting as easy as possible. As he remarked to me, "At my time of life freedom from physical pain is a very important matter."

It must not be imagined that he was a wearisome hypochondriac. He was really much too well-bred to be a nuisance. He had an eye for the small weaknesses of humanity. But it was a good-natured eye. He made a restful, easy, pleasant companion for the hours between dinner and bedtime. We spent three evenings together, and then I had to leave Naples in a hurry to look after a friend who had fallen seriously ill in Taormina. Having nothing to do, *Il Conde* came to see me off at the station. I was somewhat upset, and his idleness was always ready to take a kindly form. He was by no means an indolent man.

He went along the train peering into the carriages for a good seat for me, and then remained talking cheerily from below. He declared he would miss me that evening very much and announced his intention of going after dinner to listen to the band in the public garden, the Villa Nazionale. He would amuse himself by hearing excellent music and looking at the best society. There would be a lot of people, as usual.

I seem to see him yet—his raised face with a friendly smile under the thick mustaches, and his kind, fatigued eyes. As the train began to move, he addressed me in two languages: first in French, saying, "*Bon voyage*"; then, in his very good, somewhat emphatic English, encouragingly, because he could see my concern: "All will—be—well—yet!"

My friend's illness having taken a decidedly favorable turn, I returned to Naples on the tenth day. I cannot say I had given much thought to *Il Conde* during my absence, but entering the dining room I looked for him in his habitual place. I had an idea he might have gone back to Sorrento to his piano and his books and his fishing. He was great friends with all the boatmen, and fished a good deal with lines from a boat. But I made out his white head in the crowd of heads, and even from a distance noticed something unusual in his attitude. Instead of sitting erect, gazing all round with alert urbanity, he drooped over his plate. I stood opposite him for some time before he looked up, a little wildly, if such a strong word can be used in connection with his correct appearance.

"Ah, my dear sir! Is it you?" he greeted me. "I hope all is well."

He was very nice about my friend. Indeed, he was always nice, with the niceness of people whose hearts are genuinely humane. But this time it cost him an effort. His attempts at general conversation broke down into dullness. It occurred to me he might have been indisposed. But before I could frame the inquiry he muttered:

"You find me here very sad."

"I am sorry for that," I said. "You haven't had bad news, I hope?"

It was very kind of me to take an interest. No. It was not that. No bad news, thank God. And he became very still as if holding his breath.

Then, leaning forward a little, and in an odd tone of awed embarrassment, he took me into his confidence.

"The truth is that I have had a very—a very—how shall I say?—abominable adventure happen to me."

The energy of the epithet was sufficiently startling in that man of moderate feelings and toned-down vocabulary. The word unpleasant I should have thought would have fitted amply the worst experience likely to befall a man of his stamp. And an adventure, too. Incredible! But it is in human nature to believe the worst; and I confess I eyed him stealthily, wondering what he had been up to. In a moment, however, my unworthy suspicions vanished. There was a fundamental refinement of nature about the man which made me dismiss all idea of some more or less disreputable scrape.

"It is very serious. Very serious." He went on, nervously. "I will tell you after dinner, if you will allow me."

I expressed my perfect acquiescence by a little bow, nothing more. I wished him to understand that I was not likely to hold him to that offer, if he thought better of it later on. We talked of indifferent things, but with a sense of difficulty quite unlike our former easy, gossipy intercourse. The hand raising a piece of bread to his lips, I noticed, trembled slightly. This symptom, in regard to my reading of the man, was no less than startling.

In the smoking room he did not hang back at all. Directly we had taken our usual seats he leaned sideways over the arm of his chair and looked straight into my eyes earnestly.

"You remember," he began, "that day you went away? I told you then I would go to the Villa Nazionale to hear some music in the evening."

I remembered. His handsome old face, so fresh for his age, unmarked by any trying experience, appeared haggard for an instant. It was like the passing of a shadow. Returning his steadfast gaze, I took a sip of my black coffee. He was systematically minute in his narrative, simply in order, I think, not to let his excitement get the better of him.

After leaving the railway station, he had an ice, and read the paper in a café. Then he went back to the hotel, dressed for dinner, and dined with a good appetite. After dinner he lingered in the hall (there were chairs and tables there) smoking his cigar; talked to the little girl of the Primo Tenore of the San Carlo theater, and exchanged a few words with that "amiable lady," the wife of the Primo Tenore. There was no performance that evening, and these people were going to the Villa also. They went out of the hotel. Very well.

At the moment of following their example—it was half-past nine already—he remembered he had a rather large sum of money in his pocketbook. He entered, therefore, the office and deposited the greater part of it with the book-keeper of the hotel. This done, he took a *carozella* and drove to the seashore. He got out of the cab and entered the Villa on foot from the Largo di Vittoria end.

He stared at me very hard. And I understood then how really impressionable he was. Every small fact and event of that evening stood out in his memory as if endowed with mystic significance. If he did not mention to me the color of the pony which drew the *carozella*, and the aspect of the man who drove, it was a mere oversight arising from his agitation, which he repressed manfully.

He had then entered the Villa Nazionale from the Largo di Vittoria end. The Villa Nazionale is a public pleasure-ground laid out in grass plots, bushes, and flower-beds between the houses of the Riviera di Chiaja and the waters of the bay. Alleys of trees, more or less parallel, stretch its whole length—which is considerable. On the Riviera di Chiaja side the electric tramcars run close to the railings. Between the garden and the sea is the fashionable drive, a broad road bordered by a low wall, beyond which the Mediterranean splashes with gentle murmurs when the weather is fine.

As life goes on late at night in Naples, the broad drive was all astir with a brilliant swarm of carriage lamps moving in pairs, some creeping slowly, others running rapidly under the thin, motionless line of electric lamps defining the shore. And a brilliant swarm of stars hung above the land humming with voices, piled up with houses, glittering with lights—and over the silent flat shadows of the sea.

The gardens themselves are not very well lit. Our friend went forward in the warm gloom, his eyes fixed upon a distant luminous region extending nearly across the whole width of the Villa, as if the air had glowed there with its own cold, bluish, and dazzling light. This magic spot, behind the black trunks of trees and masses of inky foliage, breathed out sweet sounds mingled with bursts of brassy roar, sudden clashes of metal, and grave, vibrating thuds.

As he walked on, all these noises combined together into a piece of elaborate music whose harmonious phrases came persuasively through a great disorderly murmur of voices and shuffling of feet on the gravel of that open space. An enormous crowd immersed in the electric light, as if in a bath of some radiant and tenuous fluid shed upon their heads by luminous globes, drifted in its hundreds round the band. Hundreds more sat on chairs in more or less concentric circles, receiving unflinchingly the great waves of sonority that ebbed out into the darkness. The Count penetrated the throng, drifted with it in tranquil enjoyment, listening and looking at the faces. All people of good society: mothers with their daughters, parents and children, young men and young women all talking, smiling, nodding to each other. Very many pretty faces, and very many pretty toilettes. There was, of course, a quantity of diverse types: showy old fellows with white mustaches, fat men, thin men, officers in uniform; but what predominated, he told me, was the South Italian type of young man, with a colorless, clear complexion, red lips, jet-black little mustache and liquid black eyes so wonderfully effective in leering or scowling.

Withdrawing from the throng, the Count shared a little table in front of the café with a young man of just such a type. Our friend had some lemonade. The young man was sitting moodily before an empty glass. He looked up once, and then looked down again. He also tilted his hat forward. Like this—

The Count made the gesture of a man pulling his hat down over his brow, and went on:

"I think to myself: he is sad; something is wrong with him; young men have their troubles. I take no notice of him, of course. I pay for my lemonade, and go away."

Strolling about in the neighborhood of the band, the Count thinks he saw twice that young man wandering alone in the crowd. Once their eyes met. It must have been the same young man, but there were so many there of that type that he could not be certain. Moreover, he was not very much concerned except in so far that he had been struck by the marked, peevish discontent of that face.

Presently, tired of the feeling of confinement one experiences in a crowd, the Count edged away from the band. An alley, very somber by contrast, presented itself invitingly with its promise of solitude and coolness. He entered it, walking slowly on till the sound of the orchestra became distinctly deadened. Then he walked back and turned about once more. He did this several times before he noticed that there was somebody occupying one of the benches.

The spot being midway between two lamp-posts the light was faint.

The man lolled back in the corner of the seat, his legs stretched out, his arms folded and his head drooping on his breast. He never stirred, as though he had fallen asleep there, but when the Count passed by next time he had changed his attitude. He sat leaning forward. His elbows were propped on his knees, and his hands were rolling a cigarette. He never looked up from that occupation.

The Count continued his stroll away from the band. He returned slowly, he said. I can imagine him enjoying to the full, but with his usual tranquillity, the balminess of this southern night and the sounds of music softened delightfully by the distance.

Presently, he approached for the third time the man on the garden seat, still leaning forward with his elbows on his knees. It was a dejected pose. In the semi-obscurity of the alley his high shirt collar and his cuffs made small patches of vivid whiteness. The Count said that he had noticed him getting up brusquely as if to walk away, but almost before he was aware of it the man stood before him asking in a low, gentle tone whether the *signore* would have the kindness to oblige him with a light.

The Count answered this request by a polite "Certainly," and dropped his hands with the intention of exploring both pockets of his trousers for the matches.

"I dropped my hands," he said, "but I never put them in my pockets. I felt a pressure there—"

He put the tip of his finger on a spot close under his breastbone, the very spot of the human body where a Japanese gentleman begins the operations of the *hara-kiri*, which is a form of suicide following upon dishonor, upon an intolerable outrage to the delicacy of one's feelings.

"I glance down," the Count continued in an awestruck voice, "and what do I see? A knife! A long knife—"

"You don't mean to say," I exclaimed, amazed, "that you have been held up like this in the Villa at half-past ten o'clock, within a stone's throw of a thousand people!"

He nodded several times, staring at me with all his might.

"The clarionet," he declared, solemnly, "was finishing his solo, and I assure you I could hear every note. Then the band crashed *fortissimo*, and that creature rolled its eyes and gnashed its teeth hissing at me with the greatest ferocity, 'Be silent! No noise or—'"

I could not get over my astonishment.

"What sort of knife was it?" I asked, stupidly.

"A long blade. A stiletto—perhaps a kitchen knife. A long narrow blade. It gleamed. And his eyes gleamed. His white teeth, too. I could see them. He was very ferocious. I thought to myself: 'If I hit him he will kill me.' How could I fight with him? He had the knife and I had nothing. I am nearly seventy, you know, and that was a young man. I seemed even to recognize him. The moody young man of the café. The young man I met in the crowd. But I could not tell. There are so many like him in this country."

The distress of that moment was reflected in his face. I should think that physically he must have been paralyzed by surprise. His thoughts, however, remained extremely active. They ranged over every alarming possibility. The idea of setting up a vigorous shouting for help occurred to him, too. But he did nothing of the kind, and the reason why he refrained gave me a good opinion of his mental self-possession. He saw in a flash that nothing prevented the other from shouting, too.

"That young man might in an instant have thrown away his knife and pretended I was the aggressor. Why not? He might have said I attacked him. Why not? It was one incredible story against another! He might have said anything—bring some dishonoring charge against me—what do I know? By his dress he was no common robber. He seemed to belong to the better classes. What could I say? He was an Italian—I am a foreigner. Of course, I have my passport, and there is our consul—but to be arrested, dragged at night to the police office like a criminal!"

He shuddered. It was in his character to shrink from scandal, much more than from mere death. And certainly for many people this would have always remained—considering certain peculiarities of Neapolitan manners—a deucedly queer story. The Count was no fool. His belief in the respectable placidity of life having received this rude shock, he thought that now anything might happen. But also a notion came into his head that this young man was perhaps merely an infuriated lunatic.

This was for me the first hint of his attitude toward this adventure. In his exaggerated delicacy of sentiment he felt that nobody's self-esteem need be affected by what a madman may choose to do to one. It became apparent, however, that the Count was to be denied that consolation. He enlarged upon the abominably savage way in which that young man rolled his glistening eyes and gnashed his white teeth. The band was going now through a slow movement of solemn braying by all the trombones, with deliberately repeated bangs of the big drum.

"But what did you do?" I asked, greatly excited.

"Nothing," answered the Count. "I let my hands hang down very still. I told him quietly I did not intend making a noise. He snarled like a dog, then said in an ordinary voice:

"'*Vostro portofolio.*'"

"So I naturally," continued the Count—and from this point acted the whole thing in pantomime. Holding me with his eyes, he went through all the motions of reaching into his inside breast pocket, taking out a pocketbook, and handing it over. But that young man, still bearing steadily on the knife, refused to touch it.

He directed the Count to take the money out himself, received it into his left hand, motioned the pocketbook to be returned to the pocket, all this being done to the sweet thrilling of flutes and clarionets sustained by the emotional drone of the hautboys. And the "young man," as the Count called him, said: "This seems very little."

"It was, indeed, only 340 or 360 lire," the Count pursued. "I had left my money in the hotel, as you know. I told him this was all I had on me. He shook his head impatiently and said:

"'*Vostro orologio.*'"

The Count gave me the dumb show of pulling out his watch, detaching it. But, as it happened, the valuable gold half-chronometer he possessed had been left at a watch-maker's for cleaning. He wore that evening (on a leather guard) the Waterbury fifty-franc thing he used to take with him on his fishing expeditions. Perceiving the nature of this booty, the well-dressed robber made a contemptuous clicking sound with his tongue like this, "Tse-Ah!" and waved it away hastily. Then, as the Count was returning the disdained object to his pocket, he demanded with a threateningly increased pressure of the knife on the epigastrium, by way of reminder:

"'*Vostri anelli.*'"

"One of the rings," went on the Count, "was given me many years ago by my wife; the other is the signet ring of my father. I said, 'No. *That* you shall not have!'"

Here the Count reproduced the gesture corresponding to that declaration by clapping one hand upon the other, and pressing both thus against his chest. It was touching in its resignation. "That you shall not have," he repeated, firmly, and closed his eyes, fully expecting—I don't know whether I am right in recording that such an unpleasant word had passed his lips—fully expecting to feel himself being—I really hesitate to say—being disembowelled by the push of the long, sharp blade resting murderously against the pit of his stomach—the very seat, in all human beings, of anguishing sensations.

Great waves of harmony went on flowing from the band.

Suddenly the Count felt the nightmarish pressure removed from the sensitive spot. He opened his eyes. He was alone. He had heard nothing. It is probable that "the young man" had departed, with light steps, some time before, but the sense of the horrid pressure had lingered even after the knife had gone. A feeling of weakness came over him. He had just time to stagger to the garden seat. He felt as though he had held his breath for a long time. He sat all in a heap, panting with the shock of the reaction.

The band was executing, with immense bravura, the complicated finale. It ended with a tremendous crash. He heard it unreal and remote, as if his ears had been stopped, and then the hard clapping of a thousand, more or less, pairs of hands, like a sudden hail-shower passing away. The profound silence which succeeded recalled him to himself.

A tramcar resembling a long glass box wherein people sat with their heads strongly lighted, ran along swiftly within sixty yards of the spot where he had been robbed. Then another rustled by, and yet another going the other way. The audience about the band had broken up, and were entering the alley in small conversing groups. The Count sat up straight and tried to think calmly of what had happened to him. The vileness of it took his breath away again. As far as I can make it out he was disgusted with himself. I do not mean to say with his behavior. Indeed, if his pantomimic rendering of it for my information was to be trusted, it was simply perfect. No, it was not that. He was not ashamed. He was shocked at being the selected victim, not of robbery so much as of contempt. His tranquillity had been wantonly desecrated. His lifelong, kindly nicety of outlook had been defaced.

Nevertheless, at that stage, before the iron had time to sink deep, he was able to argue himself into comparative equanimity. As his agitation calmed down somewhat, he became aware that he was frightfully hungry. Yes, hungry. The sheer emotion had made him simply ravenous. He left the seat and, after walking for some time, found himself outside the gardens and before an arrested tramcar, without knowing very well how he came there. He got in as if in a dream, by a sort of instinct. Fortunately he found in his trouser pocket a copper to satisfy the conductor. Then the car stopped, and as everybody was getting out he got out, too. He recognized the Piazza San Ferdinando, but apparently it did not occur to him to take a cab and drive to the hotel. He remained in distress on the Piazza like a lost dog, thinking vaguely of the best way of getting something to eat at once.

Suddenly he remembered his twenty-franc piece. He explained to me that he had that piece of French gold for something like three years. He used to carry it about with him as a sort of reserve in case of accident. Anybody is liable to have his pocket picked—a quite different thing from a brazen and insulting robbery.

The monumental arch of the Galleria Umberto faced him at the top of a noble flight of stairs. He climbed these without loss of time, and directed his steps toward the Café Umberto. All the tables outside were occupied by a lot of people who were drinking. But as he wanted something to eat, he went inside into the café, which is divided into aisles by square pillars set all round with long looking-glasses. The Count sat down on a red plush bench against one of these pillars, waiting for his risotto. And his mind reverted to his abominable adventure.

He thought of the moody, well-dressed young man, with whom he had exchanged glances in the crowd around the bandstand, and who, he felt confident, was the robber. Would he recognize him again? Doubtless. But he did not want ever to see him again. The best thing was to forget this humiliating episode.

The Count looked round anxiously for the coming of his risotto, and, behold! to the left against the wall—there sat the young man. He was alone at a table, with a bottle of some sort of wine or syrup and a carafe of iced water before him. The smooth olive cheeks, the red lips, the little jet-black mustache turned up gallantly, the fine black eyes a little heavy and shaded by long eyelashes, that peculiar expression of cruel discontent to be seen only in the busts of some Roman emperors—it was he, no doubt at all. But that was a type. The Count looked away hastily. The young officer over there reading a paper was like that, too. Same type. Two young men farther away playing draughts also resembled—

The Count lowered his head with the fear in his heart of being everlastingly haunted by the vision of that young man. He began to eat his risotto. Presently he heard the young man on his left call the waiter in a bad-tempered tone.

At the call, not only his own waiter, but two other idle waiters belonging to a quite different row of tables, rushed toward him with obsequious alacrity, which is not the general characteristic of the waiters in the Café Umberto. The young man muttered something and one of the waiters walking rapidly to the nearest door called out into the Galleria: "Pasquale! O! Pasquale!"

Everybody knows Pasquale, the shabby old fellow who, shuffling between the tables, offers for sale cigars, cigarettes, picture postcards, and matches to the clients of the café. He is in many respects an engaging scoundrel. The Count saw the gray-haired, unshaven ruffian enter the café, the glass case hanging from his neck by a leather strap, and, at a word from the waiter, make his shuffling way with a sudden spurt to the young man's table. The young man was in need of a cigar with which Pasquale served him fawningly. The old pedlar was going out, when the Count, on a sudden impulse, beckoned to him.

Pasquale approached, the smile of deferential recognition combining oddly with the cynical searching expression of his eyes. Leaning his case on the table, he lifted the glass lid without a word. The Count took a box of cigarettes and urged by a fearful curiosity, asked as casually as he could—

"Tell me, Pasquale, who is that young *signore* sitting over there?"

The other bent over his box confidentially.

"That, *Signor Conde*," he said, beginning to rearrange his wares busily and without looking up, "that is a young *cavaliere* of a very good family from Bari. He studies in the University here, and is the chief, *capo*, of an association of young men—of very nice young men."

He paused, and then, with mingled discretion and pride of knowledge, murmured the explanatory word "Camorra" and shut down the lid. "A very powerful Camorra," he breathed out. "The professors themselves respect it greatly . . . *una lira e cinquanti centesimi, Signor Conde.*"

Our friend paid with the gold piece. While Pasquale was making up the change, he observed that the young man, of whom he had heard so much in a few words, was watching the transaction covertly. After the old vagabond had withdrawn with a bow, the Count settled with the waiter and sat still. A numbness, he told me, had come over him.

The young man paid, too, got up, and crossed over, apparently for the purpose of looking at himself in the mirror set in the pillar nearest to the Count's seat. He was dressed all in black with a dark green bow tie. The Count looked round, and was startled by meeting a vicious glance out of the corners of the other's eyes. The young *cavaliere* from Bari (according to Pasquale; but Pasquale is, of course, an accomplished liar) went on arranging his tie, settling his hat before the glass, and meantime he spoke just loud enough to be heard by the Count. He spoke through his teeth with the most insulting venom of contempt and gazing straight into the mirror.

"Ah! So you had some gold on you—you old liar—you old *birba*—you *furfante*! But you are not done with me yet."

The fiendishness of his expression vanished like lightning, and he lounged out of the café with a moody, impassive face.

The poor Count, after telling me this last episode, fell back trembling in his chair. His forehead broke into perspiration. There was a wanton insolence in the spirit of this outrage which appalled even me. What it was to the Count's delicacy I won't attempt to guess. I am sure that if he had been not too refined to do such a blatantly vulgar thing as dying from apoplexy in a café, he would have had a fatal stroke there and then. All irony apart, my difficulty was to keep him from seeing the full extent of my commiseration. He shrank from every excessive sentiment, and my commiseration was practically unbounded. It did not surprise me to hear that he had been in bed a week. He had got up to make his arrangements for leaving Southern Italy for good and all.

And the man was convinced that he could not live through a whole year in any other climate!

No argument of mine had any effect. It was not timidity, though he did say to me once: "You do not know what a Camorra is, my dear sir. I am a marked man." He was not afraid of what could be done to him. His delicate conception of his dignity was defiled by a degrading experience. He couldn't stand that. No Japanese gentleman, outraged in his exaggerated sense of honor, could have gone about his preparations for *hara-kiri* with greater resolution. To go home really amounted to suicide for the poor Count.

There is a saying of Neapolitan patriotism, intended for the information of foreigners, I presume: "See Naples and then die." *Vedi Napoli e poi mori.* It is a saying of excessive vanity, and everything excessive was abhorrent to the nice moderation of the poor Count. Yet, as I was seeing him off at the railway station, I thought he was behaving with singular fidelity to its conceited spirit. *Vedi Napoli*! . . . He had seen it! He had seen it with startling thoroughness—and now he was going to his grave. He was going to it by the *train de luxe* of the International Sleeping Car Company, via Trieste and Vienna. As the four long, somber coaches pulled out of the station I raised my hat with the solemn feeling of paying the last tribute of respect to a funeral *cortège*. *Il Conde*'s profile, much aged already, glided away from me in stony immobility, behind the lighted pane of glass—*Vedi Napoli e poi mori*!

A SMILE OF FORTUNE

EVER SINCE THE sun rose I had been looking ahead. The ship glided gently in smooth water. After a sixty days' passage I was anxious to make my landfall, a fertile and beautiful island of the tropics. The more enthusiastic of its inhabitants delight in describing it as the "Pearl of the Ocean." Well, let us call it the "*Pearl*." It's a good name. A pearl distilling much sweetness upon the world.

This is only a way of telling you that first-rate sugar-cane is grown there. All the population of the *Pearl* lives for it and by it. Sugar is their daily bread, as it were. And I was coming to them for a cargo of sugar in the hope of the crop having been good and of the freights being high.

Mr. Burns, my chief mate, made out the land first; and very soon I became entranced by this blue, pinnacled apparition, almost transparent against the light of the sky, a mere emanation, the astral body of an island risen to greet me from afar. It is a rare phenomenon, such a sight of the *Pearl* at sixty miles off. And I wondered half seriously whether it was a good omen, whether what would meet me in that island would be as luckily exceptional as this beautiful, dreamlike vision so very few seamen have been privileged to behold.

But horrid thoughts of business interfered with my enjoyment of an accomplished passage. I was anxious for success and I wished, too, to do justice to the flattering latitude of my owners' instructions contained in one noble phrase: "We leave it to you to do the best you can with the ship." . . . All the world being thus given me for a stage, my abilities appeared to me no bigger than a pinhead.

Meantime the wind dropped, and Mr. Burns began to make disagreeable remarks about my usual bad luck. I believe it was his devotion for me which made him critically outspoken on every occasion. All the same, I would not have put up with his humors if it had not been my lot at one time to nurse him through a desperate illness at sea. After snatching him out of the jaws of death, so to speak, it would have been absurd to throw away such an efficient officer. But sometimes I wished he would dismiss himself.

We were late in closing in with the land, and had to anchor outside the harbor till next day. An unpleasant and unrestful night followed. In this roadstead, strange to us both, Burns and I remained on deck almost all the time. Clouds swirled down the porphyry crags under which we lay. The rising wind made a great bullying noise among the naked spars, with interludes of sad moaning. I remarked that we had been in luck to fetch the anchorage before dark. It would have been a nasty, anxious night to hang off a harbor under canvas. But my chief mate was uncompromising in his attitude.

"Luck, you call it, sir! Ay—our usual luck. The sort of luck to thank God it's no worse!" And so he fretted through the dark hours, while I drew on my fund of philosophy. Ah, but it was an exasperating, weary, endless night, to be lying at anchor close under that black coast! The agitated water made snarling sounds all round the ship. At times a wild gust of wind out of a gully high up on the cliffs struck on our rigging a harsh and plaintive note like the wail of a forsaken soul.

Chapter 1

By half-past seven in the morning, the ship being then inside the harbor at last and moored within a long stone's-throw from the quay, my stock of philosophy was nearly exhausted. I was dressing hurriedly in my cabin when the steward came tripping in with a morning suit over his arm.

Hungry, tired, and depressed, with my head engaged inside a white shirt irritatingly stuck together by too much starch, I desired him peevishly to "heave round with that breakfast." I wanted to get ashore as soon as possible.

"Yes, sir. Ready at eight, sir. There's a gentleman from the shore waiting to speak to you, sir." This statement was curiously slurred over. I dragged the shirt violently over my head and emerged staring.

"So early!" I cried. "Who's he? What does he want?" On coming in from sea one has to pick up the conditions of an utterly unrelated existence. Every little event at first has the peculiar emphasis of novelty. I was greatly surprised by that early caller; but there was no reason for my steward to look so particularly foolish.

"Didn't you ask for the name?" I inquired in a stern tone.

"His name's Jacobus, I believe," he mumbled shamefacedly.

"Mr. Jacobus!" I exclaimed loudly, more surprised than ever, but with a total change of feeling. "Why couldn't you say so at once?" But the fellow had scuttled out of my room. Through the momentarily opened door I had a glimpse of a tall, stout man standing in the cuddy by the table on which the cloth was already laid; a "harbor" table-cloth, stainless and dazzlingly white. So far good.

I shouted courteously through the closed door, that I was dressing and would be with him in a moment. In return the assurance that there was no hurry reached me in the visitor's deep, quiet undertone. His time was my own. He dared say I would give him a cup of coffee presently.

"I am afraid you will have a poor breakfast," I cried apologetically. "We have been sixty-one days at sea, you know." A quiet little laugh, with a "That'll be all right, Captain," was his answer. All this, words, intonation, the glimpsed attitude of the man in the cuddy, had an unexpected character, a something friendly in it—propitiatory. And my surprise was not diminished thereby. What did this call mean? Was it the sign of some dark design against my commercial innocence? Ah! These commercial interests—spoiling the finest life under the sun. Why must the sea be used for trade—and for war as well? Why kill and traffic on it, pursuing selfish aims of no great importance after all? It would have been so much nicer just to sail about with here and there a port and a bit of land to stretch one's legs on, buy a few books, and get a change of cooking for a while. But, living in a world more or less homicidal and desperately mercantile, it was plainly my duty to make the best of its opportunities.

My owners' letter had left it to me, as I have said before, to do my best for the ship, according to my own judgment. But it contained also a postscript worded somewhat as follows:

"Without meaning to interfere with your liberty of action we are writing by the outgoing mail to some of our business friends there who may be of assistance to you. We desire you particularly to call on Mr. Jacobus, a prominent merchant and charterer. Should you hit it off with him he may be able to put you in the way of profitable employment for the ship."

Hit it off! Here was the prominent creature absolutely on board asking for the favor of a cup of coffee! And life not being a fairy-tale the improbability of the event almost shocked me. Had I discovered an enchanted nook of the earth where wealthy merchants rush fasting on board ships before they are fairly moored? Was this white magic or merely some black trick of trade? I came in the end (while making the bow of my tie) to suspect that perhaps I did not get the name right. I had been thinking of the prominent Mr. Jacobus pretty frequently during the passage and my hearing might have been deceived by some remote similarity of sound. . . The steward might have said Antrobus—or maybe Jackson.

But coming out of my stateroom with an interrogative "Mr. Jacobus?" I was met by a quiet "Yes," uttered with a gentle smile. The "yes" was rather perfunctory. He did not seem to make much of the fact that he was Mr. Jacobus. I took stock of a big, pale face, hair thin on the top, whiskers also thin, of a faded nondescript color, heavy eyelids. The thick, smooth lips in repose looked as if glued together. The smile was faint. A heavy, tranquil man. I named my two officers, who just then came down to breakfast; but why Mr. Burns's silent demeanor should suggest suppressed indignation I could not understand.

While we were taking our seats round the table some disconnected words of an altercation going on in the companionway reached my ear. A stranger apparently wanted to come down to interview me, and the steward was opposing him.

"You can't see him."

"Why can't I?"

"The Captain is at breakfast, I tell you. He'll be going on shore presently, and you can speak to him on deck."

"That's not fair. You let—"

"I've had nothing to do with that."

"Oh, yes, you have. Everybody ought to have the same chance. You let that fellow—"

The rest I lost. The person having been repulsed successfully, the steward came down. I can't say he looked flushed—he was a mulatto—but he looked flustered. After putting the dishes on the table he remained by the sideboard with that lackadaisical air of indifference he used to assume when he had done something too clever by half and was afraid of getting into a scrape over it. The contemptuous expression of Mr. Burns's face as he looked from him to me was really extraordinary. I couldn't imagine what new bee had stung the mate now.

The Captain being silent, nobody else cared to speak, as is the way in ships. And I was saying nothing simply because I had been made dumb by the splendor of the entertainment. I had expected the usual sea-breakfast, whereas I beheld spread before us a veritable feast of shore provisions: eggs, sausages, butter which plainly did not come from a Danish tin, cutlets, and even a dish of potatoes. It was three weeks since

I had seen a real, live potato. I contemplated them with interest, and Mr. Jacobus disclosed himself as a man of human, homely sympathies, and something of a thought-reader.

"Try them, Captain," he encouraged me in a friendly undertone. "They are excellent."

"They look that," I admitted. "Grown on the island, I suppose."

"Oh, no, imported. Those grown here would be more expensive."

I was grieved at the ineptitude of the conversation. Were these the topics for a prominent and wealthy merchant to discuss? I thought the simplicity with which he made himself at home rather attractive; but what is one to talk about to a man who comes on one suddenly, after sixty-one days at sea, out of a totally unknown little town in an island one has never seen before? What were (besides sugar) the interests of that crumb of the earth, its gossip, its topics of conversation? To draw him on business at once would have been almost indecent—or even worse: impolitic. All I could do at the moment was to keep on in the old groove.

"Are the provisions generally dear here?" I asked, fretting inwardly at my inanity.

"I wouldn't say that," he answered placidly, with that appearance of saving his breath his restrained manner of speaking suggested.

He would not be more explicit, yet he did not evade the subject. Eyeing the table in a spirit of complete abstemiousness (he wouldn't let me help him to any eatables) he went into details of supply. The beef was for the most part imported from Madagascar; mutton of course was rare and somewhat expensive, but good goat's flesh—

"Are these goat's cutlets?" I exclaimed hastily, pointing at one of the dishes.

Posed sentimentally by the sideboard, the steward gave a start.

"Lor', no, sir! It's real mutton!" Mr. Burns got through his breakfast impatiently, as if exasperated by being made a party to some monstrous foolishness, muttered a curt excuse, and went on deck. Shortly afterwards the second mate took his smooth red countenance out of the cabin. With the appetite of a schoolboy, and after two months of sea-fare, he appreciated the generous spread. But I did not. It smacked of extravagance. All the same, it was a remarkable feat to have produced it so quickly, and I congratulated the steward on his smartness in a somewhat ominous tone. He gave me a deprecatory smile and, in a way I didn't know what to make of, blinked his fine dark eyes in the direction of the guest.

The latter asked under his breath for another cup of coffee, and nibbled ascetically at a piece of very hard ship's biscuit. I don't think he consumed a square inch in the end; but meantime he gave me, casually as it were, a complete account of the sugar crop, of the local business houses, of the state of the freight market. All that talk was interspersed with hints as to personalities, amounting to veiled warnings, but his pale, fleshy face remained equable, without a gleam, as if ignorant of his voice. As you may imagine I opened my ears very wide. Every word was precious. My ideas as to the value of business friendship were being favorably modified. He gave me the names of all the disponible ships together with their tonnage and the names of their commanders. From that, which was still commercial information, he condescended to mere harbor gossip. The Hilda had unaccountably lost her figurehead in the Bay of Bengal, and her captain was greatly affected by this. He and the ship had been getting on in years together and the old gentleman imagined this strange event to be the forerunner of his own early dissolution. The Stella had experienced awful weather off the Cape—had her decks swept, and the chief officer washed overboard. And only a few hours before reaching port the baby died.

Poor Captain H- and his wife were terribly cut up. If they had only been able to bring it into port alive it could have been probably saved; but the wind failed them for the last week or so, light breezes, and . . . the baby was going to be buried this afternoon. He supposed I would attend—

"Do you think I ought to?" I asked, shrinkingly.

He thought so, decidedly. It would be greatly appreciated. All the captains in the harbor were going to attend. Poor Mrs. H- was quite prostrated. Pretty hard on H- altogether.

"And you, Captain—you are not married I suppose?"

"No, I am not married," I said. "Neither married nor even engaged."

Mentally I thanked my stars; and while he smiled in a musing, dreamy fashion, I expressed my acknowledgments for his visit and for the interesting business information he had been good enough to impart to me. But I said nothing of my wonder thereat.

"Of course, I would have made a point of calling on you in a day or two," I concluded.

He raised his eyelids distinctly at me, and somehow managed to look rather more sleepy than before.

"In accordance with my owners' instructions," I explained. "You have had their letter, of course?"

By that time he had raised his eyebrows too but without any particular emotion. On the contrary he struck me then as absolutely imperturbable.

"Oh! You must be thinking of my brother."

It was for me, then, to say "Oh!" But I hope that no more than civil surprise appeared in my voice when I asked him to what, then, I owed the pleasure. . . . He was reaching for an inside pocket leisurely.

"My brother's a very different person. But I am well known in this part of the world. You've probably heard—"

I took a card he extended to me. A thick business card, as I lived! Alfred Jacobus—the other was Ernest—dealer in every description of ship's stores! Provisions salt and fresh, oils, paints, rope, canvas, etcetera, etcetera. Ships in harbor victualled by contract on moderate terms—

"I've never heard of you," I said brusquely.

His low-pitched assurance did not abandon him.

"You will be very well satisfied," he breathed out quietly.

I was not placated. I had the sense of having been circumvented somehow. Yet I had deceived myself—if there was any deception. But the confounded cheek of inviting himself to breakfast was enough to deceive anyone. And the thought struck me: Why! The fellow had provided all these eatables himself in the way of business. I said:

"You must have got up mighty early this morning."

He admitted with simplicity that he was on the quay before six o'clock waiting for my ship to come in. He gave me the impression that it would be impossible to get rid of him now.

"If you think we are going to live on that scale," I said, looking at the table with an irritated eye, "you are jolly well mistaken."

"You'll find it all right, Captain. I quite understand."

Nothing could disturb his equanimity. I felt dissatisfied, but I could not very well fly out at him. He had told me many useful things—and besides he was the brother of that wealthy merchant. That seemed queer enough.

I rose and told him curtly that I must now go ashore. At once he offered the use of his boat for all the time of my stay in port.

"I only make a nominal charge," he continued equably. "My man remains all day at the landing-steps. You have only to blow a whistle when you want the boat."

And, standing aside at every doorway to let me go through first, he carried me off in his custody after all. As we crossed the quarter-deck two shabby individuals stepped forward and in mournful silence offered me business cards which I took from them without a word under his heavy eye. It was a useless and gloomy ceremony. They were the touts of the other ship-chandlers, and he placid at my back, ignored their existence.

We parted on the quay, after he had expressed quietly the hope of seeing me often "at the store." He had a smoking room for captains there, with newspapers and a box of "rather decent cigars." I left him very unceremoniously.

My consignees received me with the usual business heartiness, but their account of the state of the freight-market was by no means so favorable as the talk of the wrong Jacobus had led me to expect. Naturally I became inclined now to put my trust in his version, rather. As I closed the door of the private office behind me I thought to myself: "H'm. A lot of lies. Commercial diplomacy. That's the sort of thing a man coming from sea has got to expect. They would try to charter the ship under the market rate."

In the big, outer room, full of desks, the chief clerk, a tall, lean, shaved person in immaculate white clothes and with a shiny, closely-cropped black head on which silvery gleams came and went, rose from his place and detained me affably. Anything they could do for me, they would be most happy. Was I likely to call again in the afternoon? What? Going to a funeral? Oh, yes, poor Captain H-.

He pulled a long, sympathetic face for a moment, then, dismissing from this workaday world the baby, which had got ill in a tempest and had died from too much calm at sea, he asked me with a dental, shark-like smile—if sharks had false teeth—whether I had yet made my little arrangements for the ship's stay in port.

"Yes, with Jacobus," I answered carelessly. "I understand he's the brother of Mr. Ernest Jacobus to whom I have an introduction from my owners."

I was not sorry to let him know I was not altogether helpless in the hands of his firm. He screwed his thin lips dubiously.

"Why," I cried, "isn't he the brother?"

"Oh, yes. . . . They haven't spoken to each other for eighteen years," he added impressively after a pause.

"Indeed! What's the quarrel about?"

"Oh, nothing! Nothing that one would care to mention," he protested primly. "He's got quite a large business. The best ship-chandler here, without a doubt. Business is all very well, but there is such a thing as personal character, too, isn't there? Good-morning, Captain."

He went away mincingly to his desk. He amused me. He resembled an old maid, a commercial old maid, shocked by some impropriety. Was it a commercial impropriety? Commercial impropriety is a serious matter, for it aims at one's pocket. Or was he only a purist in conduct who disapproved of Jacobus doing his own touting? It was certainly undignified. I wondered how the merchant brother liked it. But then different countries, different customs. In a community so isolated and so exclusively "trading" social standards have their own scale.

Chapter 2

I WOULD HAVE gladly dispensed with the mournful opportunity of becoming acquainted by sight with all my fellow-captains at once. However I found my way to the cemetery. We made a considerable group of bareheaded men in somber garments. I noticed that those of our company most approaching to the now obsolete sea-dog type were the most moved—perhaps because they had less "manner" than the new generation. The old sea-dog, away from his natural element, was a simple and sentimental animal. I noticed one—he was facing me across the grave—who was dropping tears. They trickled down his weather-beaten face like drops of rain on an old rugged wall. I learned afterwards that he was looked upon as the terror of sailors, a hard man; that he had never had wife or chick of his own, and that, engaged from his tenderest years in deep-sea voyages, he knew women and children merely by sight.

Perhaps he was dropping those tears over his lost opportunities, from sheer envy of paternity and in strange jealousy of a sorrow which he could never know. Man, and even the sea-man, is a capricious animal, the creature and the victim of lost opportunities. But he made me feel ashamed of my callousness. I had no tears.

I listened with horribly critical detachment to that service I had had to read myself, once or twice, over childlike men who had died at sea. The words of hope and defiance, the winged words so inspiring in the free immensity of water and sky, seemed to fall wearily into the little grave. What was the use of asking Death where her sting was, before that small, dark hole in the ground? And then my thoughts escaped me altogether—away into matters of life—and no very high matters at that—ships, freights, business. In the instability of his emotions man resembles deplorably a monkey. I was disgusted with my thoughts—and I thought: Shall I be able to get a charter soon? Time's money. . . . Will that Jacobus really put good business in my way? I must go and see him in a day or two.

Don't imagine that I pursued these thoughts with any precision. They pursued me rather: vague, shadowy, restless, shamefaced. Theirs was a callous, abominable, almost revolting, pertinacity. And it was the presence of that pertinacious ship-chandler which had started them. He stood mournfully among our little band of men from the sea, and I was angry at his presence, which, suggesting his brother the merchant, had caused me to become outrageous to myself. For indeed I had preserved some decency of feeling. It was only the mind which—It was over at last. The poor father—a man of forty with black, bushy side-whiskers and a pathetic gash on his freshly-shaved chin—thanked us all, swallowing his tears. But for some reason, either because I lingered at the gate of the cemetery being somewhat hazy as to my way back, or because I was the youngest, or ascribing my moodiness caused by remorse to some more worthy and appropriate sentiment, or simply because I was even more of a stranger to him than the others—he singled me out. Keeping at my side, he renewed his thanks, which I listened to in a gloomy, conscience-stricken silence. Suddenly he slipped one hand under my arm and waved the other after a tall, stout figure walking away by itself down a street in a flutter of thin, gray garments:

"That's a good fellow—a real good fellow"—he swallowed down a belated sob—"this Jacobus."

And he told me in a low voice that Jacobus was the first man to board his ship on arrival, and, learning of their misfortune, had taken charge of everything, volunteered to attend to all routine business, carried off the ship's papers on shore, arranged for the funeral—

"A good fellow. I was knocked over. I had been looking at my wife for ten days. And helpless. Just you think of that! The dear little chap died the very day we made the land. How I managed to take the ship in God alone knows! I couldn't see anything; I couldn't speak; I couldn't. . . . You've heard, perhaps, that we lost our mate overboard on the passage? There was no one to do it for me. And the poor woman nearly crazy down below there all alone with the . . . By the Lord! It isn't fair."

We walked in silence together. I did not know how to part from him. On the quay he let go my arm and struck fiercely his fist into the palm of his other hand.

"By God, it isn't fair!" he cried again. "Don't you ever marry unless you can chuck the sea first. . . . It isn't fair."

I had no intention to "chuck the sea," and when he left me to go aboard his ship I felt convinced that I would never marry. While I was waiting at the steps for Jacobus's boatman, who had gone off somewhere, the captain of the Hilda joined me, a slender silk umbrella in his hand and the sharp points of his archaic, Gladstonian shirt-collar framing a small, clean-shaved, ruddy face. It was wonderfully fresh for his age, beautifully modelled and lit up by remarkably clear blue eyes. A lot of white hair, glossy like spun glass, curled upwards slightly under the brim of his valuable, ancient, panama hat with a broad black ribbon. In the aspect of that vivacious, neat, little old man there was something quaintly angelic and also boyish.

He accosted me, as though he had been in the habit of seeing me every day of his life from my earliest childhood, with a whimsical remark on the appearance of a stout negro woman who was sitting upon a stool near the edge of the quay. Presently he observed amiably that I had a very pretty little barque.

I returned this civil speech by saying readily:

"Not so pretty as the Hilda."

At once the corners of his clear-cut, sensitive mouth dropped dismally.

"Oh, dear! I can hardly bear to look at her now."

Did I know, he asked anxiously, that he had lost the figurehead of his ship; a woman in a blue tunic edged with gold, the face perhaps not so very, very pretty, but her bare white arms beautifully shaped and extended as if she were swimming? Did I? Who would have expected such a things . . . After twenty years, too!

Nobody could have guessed from his tone that the woman was made of wood; his trembling voice, his agitated manner gave to his lamentations a ludicrously scandalous flavor. . . . Disappeared at night—a clear fine night with just a slight swell—in the gulf of Bengal. Went off without a splash; no one in the ship could tell why, how, at what hour—after twenty years last October. . . . Did I ever hear! . . .

I assured him sympathetically that I had never heard—and he became very doleful. This meant no good he was sure. There was something in it which looked like a warning. But when I remarked that surely another figure of a woman could be procured I found myself being soundly rated for my levity. The old boy flushed pink under his clear tan as if I had proposed something improper. One could replace masts, I was told, or a lost rudder—any working part of a ship; but where was the use of sticking up a new figurehead? What satisfaction? How could one care for it? It was easy to see that I had never been shipmates with a figurehead for over twenty years.

"A new figurehead!" he scolded in unquenchable indignation. "Why! I've been a widower now for eight-and-twenty years come next May and I would just as soon think of getting a new wife. You're as bad as that fellow Jacobus."

I was highly amused.

"What has Jacobus done? Did he want you to marry again, Captain?" I inquired in a deferential tone. But he was launched now and only grinned fiercely.

"Procure—indeed! He's the sort of chap to procure you anything you like for a price. I hadn't been moored here for an hour when he got on board and at once offered to sell me a figurehead he happens to have in his yard somewhere. He got Smith, my mate, to talk to me about it. 'Mr. Smith,' says I, 'don't you know me better than that? Am I the sort that would pick up with another man's cast-off figurehead?' And after all these years, too! The way some of you young fellows talk—"

I affected great compunction, and as I stepped into the boat I said soberly:

"Then I see nothing for it but to fit in a neat fiddlehead—perhaps. You know, carved scrollwork, nicely gilt."

He became very dejected after his outburst.

"Yes. Scrollwork. Maybe. Jacobus hinted at that, too. He's never at a loss when there's any money to be extracted from a sailorman. He would make me pay through the nose for that carving. A gilt fiddlehead did you say—eh? I dare say it would do for you. You young fellows don't seem to have any feeling for what's proper."

He made a convulsive gesture with his right arm.

"Never mind. Nothing can make much difference. I would just as soon let the old thing go about the world with a bare cutwater," he cried sadly. Then as the boat got away from the steps he raised his voice on the edge of the quay with comical animosity:

"I would! If only to spite that figurehead-procuring bloodsucker. I am an old bird here and don't you forget it. Come and see me on board some day!"

I spent my first evening in port quietly in my ship's cuddy; and glad enough was I to think that the shore life which strikes one as so pettily complex, discordant, and so full of new faces on first coming from sea, could be kept off for a few hours longer. I was however fated to hear the Jacobus note once more before I slept.

Mr. Burns had gone ashore after the evening meal to have, as he said, "a look round." As it was quite dark when he announced his intention I didn't ask him what it was he expected to see. Some time about midnight, while sitting with a book in the saloon, I heard cautious movements in the lobby and hailed him by name.

Burns came in, stick and hat in hand, incredibly vulgarized by his smart shore togs, with a jaunty air and an odious twinkle in his eye. Being asked to sit down he laid his hat and stick on the table and after we had talked of ship affairs for a little while:

"I've been hearing pretty tales on shore about that ship-chandler fellow who snatched the job from you so neatly, sir."

I remonstrated with my late patient for his manner of expressing himself. But he only tossed his head disdainfully. A pretty dodge indeed: boarding a strange ship with breakfast in two baskets for all hands and calmly inviting himself to the captain's table! Never heard of anything so crafty and so impudent in his life.

I found myself defending Jacobus's unusual methods.

"He's the brother of one of the wealthiest merchants in the port." The mate's eyes fairly snapped green sparks.

"His grand brother hasn't spoken to him for eighteen or twenty years," he declared triumphantly. "So there!"

"I know all about that," I interrupted loftily.

"Do you sir? H'm!" His mind was still running on the ethics of commercial competition. "I don't like to see your good nature taken advantage of. He's bribed that steward of ours with a five-rupee note to let him come down—or ten for that matter. He don't care. He will shove that and more into the bill presently."

"Is that one of the tales you have heard ashore?" I asked.

He assured me that his own sense could tell him that much. No; what he had heard on shore was that no respectable person in the whole town would come near Jacobus. He lived in a large old-fashioned house in one of the quiet streets with a big garden. After telling me this Burns put on a mysterious air. "He keeps a girl shut up there who, they say—"

"I suppose you've heard all this gossip in some eminently respectable place?" I snapped at him in a most sarcastic tone.

The shaft told, because Mr. Burns, like many other disagreeable people, was very sensitive himself. He remained as if thunderstruck, with his mouth open for some further communication, but I did not give him the chance. "And, anyhow, what the deuce do I care?" I added, retiring into my room.

And this was a natural thing to say. Yet somehow I was not indifferent. I admit it is absurd to be concerned with the morals of one's ship-chandler, if ever so well connected; but his personality had stamped itself upon my first day in harbor, in the way you know.

After this initial exploit Jacobus showed himself anything but intrusive. He was out in a boat early every morning going round the ships he served, and occasionally remaining on board one of them for breakfast with the captain.

As I discovered that this practice was generally accepted, I just nodded to him familiarly when one morning, on coming out of my room, I found him in the cabin. Glancing over the table I saw that his place was already laid. He stood awaiting my appearance, very bulky and placid, holding a beautiful bunch of flowers in his thick hand. He offered them to my notice with a faint, sleepy smile. From his own garden; had a very fine old garden; picked them himself that morning before going out to business; thought I would like. . . . He turned away. "Steward, can you oblige me with some water in a large jar, please."

I assured him jocularly, as I took my place at the table, that he made me feel as if I were a pretty girl, and that he mustn't be surprised if I blushed. But he was busy arranging his floral tribute at the sideboard. "Stand it before the Captain's plate, steward, please." He made this request in his usual undertone.

The offering was so pointed that I could do no less than to raise it to my nose, and as he sat down noiselessly he breathed out the opinion that a few flowers improved notably the appearance of a ship's saloon. He wondered why I did not have a shelf fitted all round the skylight for flowers in pots to take with me to sea. He had a skilled workman able to fit up shelves in a day, and he could procure me two or three dozen good plants—

The tips of his thick, round fingers rested composedly on the edge of the table on each side of his cup of coffee. His face remained immovable. Mr. Burns was smiling maliciously to himself. I declared that I hadn't the slightest intention of turning my skylight into a conservatory only to keep the cabin-table in a perpetual mess of mold and dead vegetable matter.

"Rear most beautiful flowers," he insisted with an upward glance. "It's no trouble really."

"Oh, yes, it is. Lots of trouble," I contradicted. "And in the end some fool leaves the skylight open in a fresh breeze, a flick of salt water gets at them and the whole lot is dead in a week."

Mr. Burns snorted a contemptuous approval. Jacobus gave up the subject passively. After a time he unglued his thick lips to ask me if I had seen his brother yet. I was very curt in my answer.

"No, not yet."

"A very different person," he remarked dreamily and got up. His movements were particularly noiseless. "Well—thank you, Captain. If anything is not to your liking please mention it to your steward. I suppose you will be giving a dinner to the office-clerks presently."

"What for?" I cried with some warmth. "If I were a steady trader to the port I could understand it. But a complete stranger! . . . I may not turn up again here for years. I don't see why! . . . Do you mean to say it is customary?"

"It will be expected from a man like you," he breathed out placidly. "Eight of the principal clerks, the manager, that's nine, you three gentlemen, that's twelve. It needn't be very expensive. If you tell your steward to give me a day's notice—"

"It will be expected of me! Why should it be expected of me? Is it because I look particularly soft—or what?"

"His immobility struck me as dignified suddenly, his imperturbable quality as dangerous. "There's plenty of time to think about that," I concluded weakly with a gesture that tried to wave him away. But before he departed he took time to mention regretfully that he had not yet had the pleasure of seeing me at his "store" to sample those cigars. He had a parcel of six thousand to dispose of, very cheap.

"I think it would be worth your while to secure some," he added with a fat, melancholy smile and left the cabin.

Mr. Burns struck his fist on the table excitedly.

"Did you ever see such impudence! He's made up his mind to get something out of you one way or another, sir."

At once feeling inclined to defend Jacobus, I observed philosophically that all this was business, I supposed. But my absurd mate, muttering broken disjointed sentences, such as: "I cannot bear! . . . Mark my words! . . ." and so on, flung out of the cabin. If I hadn't nursed him through that deadly fever I wouldn't have suffered such manners for a single day.

Chapter 3

Jacobus having put me in mind of his wealthy brother I concluded I would pay that business call at once. I had by that time heard a little more of him. He was a member of the Council, where he made himself objectionable to the authorities. He exercised a considerable influence on public opinion. Lots of people owed him money. He was an importer on a great scale of all sorts of goods. For instance, the whole supply of bags for sugar was practically in his hands. This last fact I did not learn till afterwards. The general impression conveyed to me was that of a local personage. He was a bachelor and gave weekly card-parties in his house out of town, which were attended by the best people in the colony.

The greater, then, was my surprise to discover his office in shabby surroundings, quite away from the business quarter, among a lot of hovels. Guided by a black board with white lettering, I climbed a narrow wooden staircase and entered a room with a bare floor of planks littered with bits of brown paper and wisps of packing straw. A great number of what looked like wine-cases were piled up against one of the walls. A lanky, inky, light-yellow, mulatto youth, miserably long-necked and generally recalling a sick chicken, got off a three-legged stool behind a cheap deal desk and faced me as if gone dumb with fright. I had some difficulty in persuading him to take in my name, though I could not get from him the nature of his objection. He did it at last with an almost agonized reluctance which ceased to be mysterious to me when I heard him being sworn at menacingly with savage, suppressed growls, then audibly cuffed and finally kicked out without any concealment whatever; because he came back flying head foremost through the door with a stifled shriek.

To say I was startled would not express it. I remained still, like a man lost in a dream. Clapping both his hands to that part of his frail anatomy which had received the shock, the poor wretch said to me simply:

"Will you go in, please." His lamentable self-possession was wonderful; but it did not do away with the incredibility of the experience. A preposterous notion that I had seen this boy somewhere before, a thing obviously impossible, was like a delicate finishing touch of weirdness added to a scene fit to raise doubts as to one's sanity. I stared anxiously about me like an awakened somnambulist.

"I say," I cried loudly, "there isn't a mistake, is there? This is Mr. Jacobus's office."

The boy gazed at me with a pained expression—and somehow so familiar! A voice within growled offensively:

"Come in, come in, since you are there. . . . I didn't know."

I crossed the outer room as one approaches the den of some unknown wild beast; with intrepidity but in some excitement. Only no wild beast that ever lived would rouse one's indignation; the power to do that belongs to the odiousness of the human brute. And I was very indignant, which did not prevent me from being at once struck by the extraordinary resemblance of the two brothers.

This one was dark instead of being fair like the other; but he was as big. He was without his coat and waistcoat; he had been doubtless snoozing in the rocking-chair which stood in a corner farthest from the window. Above the great bulk of his crumpled white shirt, buttoned with three diamond studs, his round face looked swarthy. It was moist; his brown mustache hung limp and ragged. He pushed a common, cane-bottomed chair toward me with his foot.

"Sit down."

I glanced at it casually, then, turning my indignant eyes full upon him, I declared in precise and incisive tones that I had called in obedience to my owners' instructions.

"Oh! Yes. H'm! I didn't understand what that fool was saying. . . . But never mind! It will teach the scoundrel to disturb me at this time of the day," he added, grinning at me with savage cynicism.

I looked at my watch. It was past three o'clock—quite the full swing of afternoon office work in the port. He snarled imperiously: "Sit down, Captain."

I acknowledged the gracious invitation by saying deliberately:

"I can listen to all you may have to say without sitting down."

Emitting a loud and vehement "Pshaw!" he glared for a moment, very round-eyed and fierce. It was like a gigantic tomcat spitting at one suddenly. "Look at him! . . . What do you fancy yourself to be? What did you come here for? If you won't sit down and talk business you had better go to the devil."

"I don't know him personally," I said. "But after this I wouldn't mind calling on him. It would be refreshing to meet a gentleman."

He followed me, growling behind my back:

"The impudence! I've a good mind to write to your owners what I think of you."

I turned on him for a moment:

"As it happens I don't care. For my part I assure you I won't even take the trouble to mention you to them."

He stopped at the door of his office while I traversed the littered anteroom. I think he was somewhat taken aback.

"I will break every bone in your body," he roared suddenly at the miserable mulatto lad, "if you ever dare to disturb me before half-past three for anybody. D'ye hear? For anybody! . . . Let alone any damned skipper," he added, in a lower growl.

The frail youngster, swaying like a reed, made a low moaning sound. I stopped short and addressed this sufferer with advice. It was prompted by the sight of a hammer (used for opening the wine-cases, I suppose) which was lying on the floor.

"If I were you, my boy, I would have that thing up my sleeve when I went in next and at the first occasion I would—"

What was there so familiar in that lad's yellow face? Entrenched and quaking behind the flimsy desk, he never looked up. His heavy, lowered eyelids gave me suddenly the clue of the puzzle. He resembled—yes, those thick glued lips—he resembled the brothers Jacobus. He resembled both, the wealthy merchant and the pushing shopkeeper (who resembled each other); he resembled them as much as a thin, light-yellow mulatto lad may resemble a big, stout, middle-aged white man. It was the exotic complexion and the slightness of his build which had put me off so completely. Now I saw in him unmistakably the Jacobus strain, weakened, attenuated, diluted as it were in a bucket of water—and I refrained from finishing my speech. I had intended to say: "Crack this brute's head for him." I still felt the conclusion to be sound. But it is no trifling responsibility to counsel parricide to anyone, however deeply injured.

"Beggarly—cheeky—skippers."

I despised the emphatic growl at my back; only, being much vexed and upset, I regret to say that I slammed the door behind me in a most undignified manner.

It may not appear altogether absurd if I say that I brought out from that interview a kindlier view of the other Jacobus. It was with a feeling resembling partisanship that, a few days later, I called at his "store." That long, cavern-like place of business, very dim at the back and stuffed full of all sorts of goods, was entered from the street by a lofty archway. At the far end I saw my Jacobus exerting himself in his shirt-sleeves among his assistants. The captains' room was a small, vaulted apartment with a stone floor and heavy iron bars in its windows like a dungeon converted to hospitable purposes. A couple of cheerful bottles and several gleaming glasses made a brilliant cluster round a tall, cool red earthenware pitcher on the center table which was littered with newspapers from all parts of the world. A well-groomed stranger in a smart gray check suit, sitting with one leg flung over his knee, put down one of these sheets briskly and nodded to me.

I guessed him to be a steamer-captain. It was impossible to get to know these men. They came and went too quickly and their ships lay moored far out, at the very entrance of the harbor. Theirs was another life altogether. He yawned slightly.

"Dull hole, isn't it?" I understood this to allude to the town.

"Do you find it so?" I murmured.

"Don't you? But I'm off tomorrow, thank goodness."

He was a very gentlemanly person, good-natured and superior. I watched him draw the open box of cigars to his side of the table, take a big cigar-case out of his pocket and begin to fill it very methodically. Presently, on our eyes meeting, he winked like a common mortal and invited me to follow his example. "They are really decent smokes." I shook my head.

"I am not off tomorrow."

"What of that? Think I am abusing old Jacobus's hospitality? Heavens! It goes into the bill, of course. He spreads such little matters all over his account. He can take care of himself! Why, it's business—"

I noted a shadow fall over his well-satisfied expression, a momentary hesitation in closing his cigar-case. But he ended by putting it in his pocket jauntily. A placid voice uttered in the doorway: "That's quite correct, Captain."

The large noiseless Jacobus advanced into the room. His quietness, in the circumstances, amounted to cordiality. He had put on his jacket before joining us, and he sat down in the chair vacated by the steamer-man, who nodded again to me and went out with a short, jarring laugh. A profound silence reigned. With his drowsy stare Jacobus seemed to be slumbering open-eyed. Yet, somehow, I was aware of being profoundly scrutinized by those heavy eyes. In the enormous cavern of the store somebody began to nail down a case, expertly: tap-tap . . . tap-tap-tap.

Two other experts, one slow and nasal, the other shrill and snappy, started checking an invoice.

"A half-coil of three-inch manila rope."

"Right!"

"Six assorted shackles."

"Right!"

"Six tins assorted soups, three of pate, two asparagus, fourteen pounds tobacco, cabin."

"Right!"

"It's for the captain who was here just now," breathed out the immovable Jacobus. "These steamer orders are very small. They pick up what they want as they go along. That man will be in Samarang in less than a fortnight. Very small orders indeed."

The calling over of the items went on in the shop; an extraordinary jumble of varied articles, paint-brushes, Yorkshire Relish, etcetera, etcetera . . . "Three sacks of best potatoes," read out the nasal voice.

At this Jacobus blinked like a sleeping man roused by a shake, and displayed some animation. At his order, shouted into the shop, a smirking half-caste clerk with his ringlets much oiled and with a pen stuck behind his ear, brought in a sample of six potatoes which he paraded in a row on the table.

Being urged to look at their beauty I gave them a cold and hostile glance. Calmly, Jacobus proposed that I should order ten or fifteen tons—tons! I couldn't believe my ears. My crew could not have eaten such a lot in a year; and potatoes (excuse these practical remarks) are a highly perishable commodity. I thought he was joking—or else trying to find out whether I was an unutterable idiot. But his purpose was not so simple. I discovered that he meant me to buy them on my own account.

"I am proposing you a bit of business, Captain. I wouldn't charge you a great price."

I told him that I did not go in for trade. I even added grimly that I knew only too well how that sort of spec generally ended.

He sighed and clasped his hands on his stomach with exemplary resignation. I admired the placidity of his impudence. Then waking up somewhat:

"Won't you try a cigar, Captain?"

"No, thanks. I don't smoke cigars."

"For once!" he exclaimed, in a patient whisper. A melancholy silence ensued. You know how sometimes a person discloses a certain unsuspected depth and acuteness of thought; that is, in other words, utters something unexpected. It was unexpected enough to hear Jacobus say:

"The man who just went out was right enough. You might take one, Captain. Here everything is bound to be in the way of business."

I felt a little ashamed of myself. The remembrance of his horrid brother made him appear quite a decent sort of fellow. It was with some compunction that I said a few words to the effect that I could have no possible objection to his hospitality.

Before I was a minute older I saw where this admission was leading me. As if changing the subject, Jacobus mentioned that his private house was about ten minutes' walk away. It had a beautiful old walled garden. Something really remarkable. I ought to come round some day and have a look at it.

He seemed to be a lover of gardens. I too take extreme delight in them; but I did not mean my compunction to carry me as far as Jacobus's flower-beds, however beautiful and old. He added, with a certain homeliness of tone:

"There's only my girl there."

It is difficult to set everything down in due order; so I must revert here to what happened a week or two before. The medical officer of the port had come on board my ship to have a look at one of my crew who was ailing, and naturally enough he was asked to step into the cabin. A fellow-shipmaster of mine was there, too; and in the conversation, somehow or other, the name of Jacobus came to be mentioned. It was pronounced with no particular reverence by the other man, I believe. I don't remember now what I was going to say. The doctor—a pleasant, cultivated fellow, with an assured manner—prevented me by striking in, in a sour tone:

"Ah! You're talking about my respected papa-in-law."

Of course, that sally silenced us at the time. But I remembered the episode, and at this juncture, pushed for something noncommittal to say, I inquired with polite surprise:

"You have your married daughter living with you, Mr. Jacobus?"

He moved his big hand from right to left quietly. No! That was another of his girls, he stated, ponderously and under his breath as usual. She . . . He seemed in a pause to be ransacking his mind for some kind of descriptive phrase. But my hopes were disappointed. He merely produced his stereotyped definition.

"She's a very different sort of person."

"Indeed. . . . And by the by, Jacobus, I called on your brother the other day. It's no great compliment if I say that I found him a very different sort of person from you."

He had an air of profound reflection, then remarked quaintly:

"He's a man of regular habits." He might have been alluding to the habit of late siesta; but I mumbled something about "beastly habits anyhow"—and left the store abruptly.

Chapter 4

My little passage with Jacobus the merchant became known generally. One or two of my acquaintances made distant allusions to it. Perhaps the mulatto boy had talked. I must confess that people appeared rather scandalized, but not with Jacobus's brutality. A man I knew remonstrated with me for my hastiness.

I gave him the whole story of my visit, not forgetting the tell-tale resemblance of the wretched mulatto boy to his tormentor. He was not surprised. No doubt, no doubt. What of that? In a jovial tone he assured me that there must be many of that sort. The elder Jacobus had been a bachelor all his life. A highly respectable bachelor. But there had never been open scandal in that connection. His life had been quite regular. It could cause no offence to anyone.

I said that I had been offended considerably. My interlocutor opened very wide eyes. Why? Because a mulatto lad got a few knocks? That was not a great affair, surely. I had no idea how insolent and untruthful these half-castes were. In fact he seemed to think Mr. Jacobus rather kind than otherwise to employ that youth at all; a sort of amiable weakness which could be forgiven.

This acquaintance of mine belonged to one of the old French families, descendants of the old colonists; all noble, all impoverished, and living a narrow domestic life in dull, dignified decay. The men, as a rule, occupy inferior posts in Government offices or in business houses. The girls are almost always pretty, ignorant of the world, kind and agreeable and generally bilingual; they prattle innocently both in French and English. The emptiness of their existence passes belief.

I obtained my entry into a couple of such households because some years before, in Bombay, I had occasion to be of use to a pleasant, ineffectual young man who was rather stranded there, not knowing what to do with himself or even how to get home to his island again. It was a matter of two hundred rupees or so, but, when I turned up, the family made a point of showing their gratitude by admitting me to their intimacy. My knowledge of the French language made me specially acceptable. They had meantime managed to marry the fellow to a woman nearly twice his age, comparatively well off: the only profession he was really fit for. But it was not all cakes and ale. The first time I called on the couple she spied a little spot of grease on the poor devil's pantaloons and made him a screaming scene of reproaches so full of sincere passion that I sat terrified as at a tragedy of Racine.

Of course there was never question of the money I had advanced him; but his sisters, Miss Angele and Miss Mary, and the aunts of both families, who spoke quaint archaic French of pre-Revolution period, and a host of distant relations adopted me for a friend outright in a manner which was almost embarrassing.

It was with the eldest brother (he was employed at a desk in my consignee's office) that I was having this talk about the merchant Jacobus. He regretted my attitude and nodded his head sagely. An influential man. One never knew when one would need him. I expressed my immense preference for the shopkeeper of the two. At that my friend looked grave.

"What on earth are you pulling that long face about?" I cried impatiently. "He asked me to see his garden and I have a good mind to go some day."

"Don't do that," he said, so earnestly that I burst into a fit of laughter; but he looked at me without a smile.

This was another matter altogether. At one time the public conscience of the island had been mightily troubled by my Jacobus. The two brothers had been partners for years in great harmony, when a wandering circus came to the island and my Jacobus became suddenly infatuated with one of the lady-riders. What made it worse was that he was married. He had not even the grace to conceal his passion. It must have been strong indeed to carry away such a large placid creature. His behavior was perfectly scandalous. He followed that woman to the Cape, and apparently traveled at the tail of that beastly circus to other parts of the world, in a most degrading position. The woman soon ceased to care for him, and treated him worse than a dog. Most extraordinary stories of moral degradation were reaching the island at that time. He had not the strength of mind to shake himself free. . . .

The grotesque image of a fat, pushing ship-chandler, enslaved by an unholy love-spell, fascinated me; and I listened rather open-mouthed to the tale as old as the world, a tale which had been the subject of legend, of moral fables, of poems, but which so ludicrously failed to fit the personality. What a strange victim for the gods! Meantime his deserted wife had died. His daughter was taken care of by his brother, who married her as advantageously as was possible in the circumstances.

"Oh! The Mrs. Doctor!" I exclaimed.

"You know that? Yes. A very able man. He wanted a lift in the world, and there was a good bit of money from her mother, besides the expectations. . . Of course, they don't know him," he added. "The doctor nods in the street, I believe, but he avoids speaking to him when they meet on board a ship, as must happen sometimes."

I remarked that this surely was an old story by now.

My friend assented. But it was Jacobus's own fault that it was neither forgiven nor forgotten. He came back ultimately. But how? Not in a spirit of contrition, in a way to propitiate his scandalized fellow-citizens. He must needs drag along with him a child—a girl. . . .

"He spoke to me of a daughter who lives with him," I observed, very much interested.

"She's certainly the daughter of the circus-woman," said my friend. "She may be his daughter, too; I am willing to admit that she is. In fact I have no doubt—"

But he did not see why she should have been brought into a respectable community to perpetuate the memory of the scandal. And that was not the worst. Presently something much more distressing happened. That abandoned woman turned up. Landed from a mail-boat. . . .

"What! Here? To claim the child perhaps," I suggested.

"Not she!" My friendly informant was very scornful. "Imagine a painted, haggard, agitated, desperate hag. Been cast off in Mozambique by somebody who paid her passage here. She had been injured internally by a kick from a horse; she hadn't a cent on her when she got ashore; I don't think she even asked to see the child. At any rate, not till the last day of her life. Jacobus hired for her a bungalow to die in. He got a couple of Sisters from the hospital to nurse her through these few months. If he didn't marry her in extremis as the good Sisters tried to bring about, it's because she wouldn't even hear of it. As the nuns said: 'The woman died impenitent.' It was reported that she ordered Jacobus out of the room with her last breath. This may be the real reason why he didn't go into mourning himself; he only put the child into black. While she was little she was to be seen sometimes about the streets attended by a negro woman, but since she became of age to put her hair up I don't think she has set foot outside that garden once. She must be over eighteen now."

Thus my friend, with some added details; such as, that he didn't think the girl had spoken to three people of any position in the island; that an elderly female relative of the brothers Jacobus had been induced by extreme poverty to accept the position of gouvernante to the girl. As to Jacobus's business (which certainly annoyed his brother) it was a wise choice on his part. It brought him in contact only with strangers of passage; whereas any other would have given rise to all sorts of awkwardness with his social equals. The man was not wanting in a certain tact—only he was naturally shameless. For why did he want to keep that girl with him? It was most painful for everybody.

I thought suddenly (and with profound disgust) of the other Jacobus, and I could not refrain from saying slyly:

"I suppose if he employed her, say, as a scullion in his household and occasionally pulled her hair or boxed her ears, the position would have been more regular—less shocking to the respectable class to which he belongs."

He was not so stupid as to miss my intention, and shrugged his shoulders impatiently.

"You don't understand. To begin with, she's not a mulatto. And a scandal is a scandal. People should be given a chance to forget. I dare say it would have been better for her if she had been turned into a scullion or something of that kind. Of course he's trying to make money in every sort of petty way, but in such a business there'll never be enough for anybody to come forward."

When my friend left me I had a conception of Jacobus and his daughter existing, a lonely pair of castaways, on a desert island; the girl sheltering in the house as if it were a cavern in a cliff, and Jacobus going out to pick up a living for both on the beach—exactly like two shipwrecked people who always hope for some rescuer to bring them back at last into touch with the rest of mankind.

But Jacobus's bodily reality did not fit in with this romantic view. When he turned up on board in the usual course, he sipped the cup of coffee placidly, asked me if I was satisfied—and I hardly listened to the harbor gossip he dropped slowly in his low, voice-saving enunciation. I had then troubles of my own. My ship chartered, my thoughts dwelling on the success of a quick round voyage, I had been suddenly confronted by a shortage of bags. A catastrophe! The stock of one special kind, called pockets, seemed to be totally exhausted. A consignment was shortly expected—it was afloat, on its way, but, meantime, the loading of my ship dead stopped, I had enough to worry about. My consignees, who had received me with such heartiness on my arrival, now, in the character of my charterers, listened to my complaints with polite helplessness. Their manager, the old-maidish, thin man, who so prudishly didn't even like to speak about the impure Jacobus, gave me the correct commercial view of the position.

"My dear Captain"—he was retracting his leathery cheeks into a condescending, shark-like smile—"we were not morally obliged to tell you of a possible shortage before you signed the charter-party. It was for you to guard against the contingency of a delay—strictly speaking. But of course we shouldn't have taken any advantage. This is no one's fault really. We ourselves have been taken unawares," he concluded primly, with an obvious lie.

This lecture I confess had made me thirsty. Suppressed rage generally produces that effect; and as I strolled on aimlessly I bethought myself of the tall earthenware pitcher in the captains' room of the Jacobus "store."

With no more than a nod to the men I found assembled there, I poured down a deep, cool draught on my indignation, then another, and then, becoming dejected, I sat plunged in cheerless reflections. The others read, talked, smoked, bandied over my head some unsubtle chaff. But my abstraction was respected. And it was without a word to anyone that I rose and went out, only to be quite unexpectedly accosted in the bustle of the store by Jacobus the outcast.

"Glad to see you, Captain. What? Going away? You haven't been looking so well these last few days, I notice. Run down, eh?"

He was in his shirt-sleeves, and his words were in the usual course of business, but they had a human note. It was commercial amenity, but I had been a stranger to amenity in that connection. I do verily believe (from the direction of his heavy glance toward a certain shelf) that he was going to suggest the purchase of Clarkson's Nerve Tonic, which he kept in stock, when I said impulsively:

"I am rather in trouble with my loading."

Wide awake under his sleepy, broad mask with glued lips, he understood at once, had a movement of the head so appreciative that I relieved my exasperation by exclaiming:

"Surely there must be eleven hundred quarter-bags to be found in the colony. It's only a matter of looking for them."

Again that slight movement of the big head, and in the noise and activity of the store that tranquil murmur:

"To be sure. But then people likely to have a reserve of quarter-bags wouldn't want to sell. They'd need that size themselves."

"That's exactly what my consignees are telling me. Impossible to buy. Bosh! They don't want to. It suits them to have the ship hung up. But if I were to discover the lot they would have to—Look here, Jacobus! You are the man to have such a thing up your sleeve."

He protested with a ponderous swing of his big head. I stood before him helplessly, being looked at by those heavy eyes with a veiled expression as of a man after some soul-shaking crisis. Then, suddenly:

"It's impossible to talk quietly here," he whispered. "I am very busy. But if you could go and wait for me in my house. It's less than ten minutes' walk. Oh, yes, you don't know the way."

He called for his coat and offered to take me there himself. He would have to return to the store at once for an hour or so to finish his business, and then he would be at liberty to talk over with me that matter of quarter-bags. This program was breathed out at me through slightly parted, still lips; his heavy, motionless glance rested upon me, placid as ever, the glance of a tired man—but I felt that it was searching, too. I could not imagine what he was looking for in me and kept silent, wondering.

"I am asking you to wait for me in my house till I am at liberty to talk this matter over. You will?"

"Why, of course!" I cried.

"But I cannot promise—"

"I dare say not," I said. "I don't expect a promise."

"I mean I can't even promise to try the move I've in my mind. One must see first . . . h'm!"

"All right. I'll take the chance. I'll wait for you as long as you like. What else have I to do in this infernal hole of a port!"

Before I had uttered my last words we had set off at a swinging pace. We turned a couple of corners and entered a street completely empty of traffic, of semi-rural aspect, paved with cobblestones nestling in grass tufts. The house came to the line of the roadway; a single story on an elevated basement of rough-stones, so that our heads were below the level of the windows as we went along. All the jalousies were tightly shut, like eyes, and the house seemed fast asleep in the afternoon sunshine. The entrance was at the side, in an alley even more grass-grown than the street: a small door, simply on the latch.

With a word of apology as to showing me the way, Jacobus preceded me up a dark passage and led me across the naked parquet floor of what I supposed to be the dining room. It was lighted by three glass doors which stood wide open on to a veranda or rather loggia running its brick arches along the garden side of the house. It was really a magnificent garden: smooth green lawns and a gorgeous maze of flower-beds in the foreground, displayed around a basin of dark water framed in a marble rim, and in the distance the massed foliage of varied trees concealing the roofs of other houses. The town might have been miles away. It was a brilliantly colored solitude, drowsing in a warm, voluptuous silence. Where the long, still shadows fell across the beds, and in shady nooks, the massed colors of the flowers had an extraordinary magnificence of effect. I stood entranced. Jacobus grasped me delicately above the elbow, impelling me to a half-turn to the left.

I had not noticed the girl before. She occupied a low, deep, wickerwork armchair, and I saw her in exact profile like a figure in a tapestry, and as motionless. Jacobus released my arm.

"This is Alice," he announced tranquilly; and his subdued manner of speaking made it sound so much like a confidential communication that I fancied myself nodding understandingly and whispering: "I see, I see." . . . Of course, I did nothing of the kind. Neither of us did anything; we stood side by side looking down at the girl. For quite a time she did not stir, staring straight before her as if watching the vision of some pageant passing through the garden in the deep, rich glow of light and the splendor of flowers.

Then, coming to the end of her reverie, she looked round and up. If I had not at first noticed her, I am certain that she too had been unaware of my presence till she actually perceived me by her father's side. The quickened upward movement of the heavy eyelids, the widening of the languid glance, passing into a fixed stare, put that beyond doubt.

Under her amazement there was a hint of fear, and then came a flash as of anger. Jacobus, after uttering my name fairly loud, said: "Make yourself at home, Captain—I won't be gone long," and went away rapidly. Before I had time to make a bow I was left alone with the girl—who, I remembered suddenly, had not been seen by any man or woman of that town since she had found it necessary to put up her hair. It looked as though it had not been touched again since that distant time of first putting up; it was a mass of black, lustrous locks, twisted anyhow high on her head, with long, untidy wisps hanging down on each side of the clear sallow face; a mass so thick and strong and abundant that, nothing but to look at, it gave you a sensation of heavy pressure on the top of your head and an impression of magnificently cynical untidiness. She leaned forward, hugging herself with crossed legs; a dingy, amber-colored, flounced wrapper of some thin stuff revealed the young supple body drawn together tensely in the deep low seat as if crouching for a spring. I detected a slight, quivering start or two, which looked uncommonly like bounding away. They were followed by the most absolute immobility.

The absurd impulse to run out after Jacobus (for I had been startled, too) once repressed, I took a chair, placed it not very far from her, sat down deliberately, and began to talk about the garden, caring not what I said, but using a gentle caressing intonation as one talks to soothe a startled wild animal. I could not even be certain that she understood me. She never raised her face nor attempted to look my way. I kept on talking only to prevent her from taking flight. She had another of those quivering, repressed starts which made me catch my breath with apprehension.

Ultimately I formed a notion that what prevented her perhaps from going off in one great, nervous leap, was the scantiness of her attire. The wicker armchair was the most substantial thing about her person. What she had on under that dingy, loose, amber wrapper must have been of the most flimsy and airy character. One could not help being aware of it. It was obvious. I felt it actually embarrassing at first; but that sort of embarrassment is got over easily by a mind not enslaved by narrow prejudices. I did not avert my gaze from Alice. I went on talking with ingratiating softness, the recollection that, most likely, she had never before been spoken to by a strange man adding to my assurance. I don't know why an emotional tenseness should have crept into the situation. But it did. And just as I was becoming aware of it a slight scream cut short my flow of urbane speech.

The scream did not proceed from the girl. It was emitted behind me, and caused me to turn my head sharply. I understood at once that the apparition in the doorway was the elderly relation of Jacobus, the companion, the gouvernante. While she remained thunderstruck, I got up and made her a low bow.

The ladies of Jacobus's household evidently spent their days in light attire. This stumpy old woman with a face like a large wrinkled lemon, beady eyes, and a shock of iron-gray hair, was dressed in a garment of some ash-colored, silky, light stuff. It fell from her thick neck down to her toes with the simplicity of an unadorned nightgown. It made her appear truly cylindrical. She exclaimed: "How did you get here?"

Before I could say a word she vanished and presently I heard a confusion of shrill protestations in a distant part of the house. Obviously no one could tell her how I got there. In a moment, with great outcries from two negro women following her, she waddled back to the doorway, infuriated.

"What do you want here?"

I turned to the girl. She was sitting straight up now, her hands posed on the arms of the chair. I appealed to her.

"Surely, Miss Alice, you will not let them drive me out into the street?"

Her magnificent black eyes, narrowed, long in shape, swept over me with an indefinable expression, then in a harsh, contemptuous voice she let fall in French a sort of explanation:

"C'est papa."

I made another low bow to the old woman.

She turned her back on me in order to drive away her black henchwomen, then surveying my person in a peculiar manner with one small eye nearly closed and her face all drawn up on that side as if with a twinge of toothache, she stepped out on the veranda, sat down in a rocking-chair some distance away, and took up her knitting from a little table. Before she started at it she plunged one of the needles into the mop of her gray hair and stirred it vigorously.

Her elementary nightgown-sort of frock clung to her ancient, stumpy, and floating form. She wore white cotton stockings and flat brown velvet slippers. Her feet and ankles were obtrusively visible on the foot-rest. She began to rock herself slightly, while she knitted. I had resumed my seat and kept quiet, for I mistrusted that old woman. What if she ordered me to depart? She seemed capable of any outrage. She had snorted once or twice; she was knitting violently.

Suddenly she piped at the young girl in French a question which I translate colloquially:

"What's your father up to, now?"

The young creature shrugged her shoulders so comprehensively that her whole body swayed within the loose wrapper; and in that unexpectedly harsh voice which yet had a seductive quality to the senses, like certain kinds of natural rough wines one drinks with pleasure:

"It's some captain. Leave me alone—will you!"

The chair rocked quicker, the old, thin voice was like a whistle.

"You and your father make a pair. He would stick at nothing—that's well known. But I didn't expect this."

I thought it high time to air some of my own French. I remarked modestly, but firmly, that this was business. I had some matters to talk over with Mr. Jacobus.

At once she piped out a derisive "Poor innocent!" Then, with a change of tone: "The shop's for business. Why don't you go to the shop to talk with him?"

The furious speed of her fingers and knitting-needles made one dizzy; and with squeaky indignation:

"Sitting here staring at that girl—is that what you call business?"

"No," I said suavely. "I call this pleasure—an unexpected pleasure. And unless Miss Alice objects—"

I half turned to her. She flung at me an angry and contemptuous "Don't care!" and leaning her elbow on her knees took her chin in her hand—a Jacobus chin undoubtedly. And those heavy eyelids, this black irritated stare reminded me of Jacobus, too—the wealthy merchant, the respected one. The design of her eyebrows also was the same, rigid and ill-omened. Yes! I traced in her a resemblance to both of them. It came to me as a sort of surprising remote inference that both these Jacobuses were rather handsome men after all. I said:

"Oh! Then I shall stare at you till you smile."

She favored me again with an even more viciously scornful "Don't care!"

The old woman broke in blunt and shrill:

"Hear his impudence! And you, too! Don't care! Go at least and put some more clothes on. Sitting there like this before this sailor riff-raff."

The sun was about to leave the *Pearl of the Ocean* for other seas, for other lands. The walled garden full of shadows blazed with color as if the flowers were giving up the light absorbed during the day. The amazing old woman became very explicit. She suggested to the girl a corset and a petticoat with a cynical unreserve which humiliated me. Was I of no more account than a wooden dummy? The girl snapped out: "Shan't!"

It was not the naughty retort of a vulgar child; it had a note of desperation. Clearly my intrusion had somehow upset the balance of their established relations. The old woman knitted with furious accuracy, her eyes fastened down on her work.

"Oh, you are the true child of your father! And THAT talks of entering a convent! Letting herself be stared at by a fellow."

"Leave off."

"Shameless thing!"

"Old sorceress," the girl uttered distinctly, preserving her meditative pose, chin in hand, and a far-away stare over the garden.

It was like the quarrel of the kettle and the pot. The old woman flew out of the chair, banged down her work, and with a great play of thick limb perfectly visible in that weird, clinging garment of hers, strode at the girl—who never stirred. I was experiencing a sort of trepidation when, as if awed by that unconscious attitude, the aged relative of Jacobus turned short upon me.

She was, I perceived, armed with a knitting-needle; and as she raised her hand her intention seemed to be to throw it at me like a dart. But she only used it to scratch her head with, examining me the while at close range, one eye nearly shut and her face distorted by a whimsical, one-sided grimace.

"My dear man," she asked abruptly, "do you expect any good to come of this?"

"I do hope so indeed, Miss Jacobus." I tried to speak in the easy tone of an afternoon caller. "You see, I am here after some bags."

"Bags! Look at that now! Didn't I hear you holding forth to that graceless wretch?"

"You would like to see me in my grave," uttered the motionless girl hoarsely.

"Grave! What about me? Buried alive before I am dead for the sake of a thing blessed with such a pretty father!" she cried; and turning to me: "You're one of these men he does business with. Well—why don't you leave us in peace, my good fellow?"

It was said in a tone—this "leave us in peace!" There was a sort of ruffianly familiarity, a superiority, a scorn in it. I was to hear it more than once, for you would show an imperfect knowledge of human nature if you thought that this was my last visit to that house—where no respectable person had put foot for ever so many years. No, you would be very much mistaken if you imagined that this reception had scared me away. First of all I was not going to run before a grotesque and ruffianly old woman.

And then you mustn't forget these necessary bags. That first evening Jacobus made me stay to dinner; after, however, telling me loyally that he didn't know whether he could do anything at all for me. He had been thinking it over. It was too difficult, he feared. . . . But he did not give it up in so many words.

We were only three at table; the girl by means of repeated "Won't!" "Shan't!" and "Don't care!" having conveyed and affirmed her intention not to come to the table, not to have any dinner, not to move from the veranda. The old relative hopped about in her flat slippers and piped indignantly, Jacobus towered over her and murmured placidly in his throat; I joined jocularly from a distance, throwing in a few words, for which under the cover of the night I received secretly a most vicious poke in the ribs from the old woman's elbow or perhaps her fist. I restrained a cry. And all the time the girl didn't even condescend to raise her head to look at any of us. All this may sound childish—and yet that stony, petulant sullenness had an obscurely tragic flavor.

And so we sat down to the food around the light of a good many candles while she remained crouching out there, staring in the dark as if feeding her bad temper on the heavily scented air of the admirable garden.

Before leaving I said to Jacobus that I would come next day to hear if the bag affair had made any progress. He shook his head slightly at that.

"I'll haunt your house daily till you pull it off. You'll be always finding me here."

His faint, melancholy smile did not part his thick lips.

"That will be all right, Captain."

Then seeing me to the door, very tranquil, he murmured earnestly the recommendation: "Make yourself at home," and also the hospitable hint about there being always "a plate of soup." It was only on my way to the quay, down the ill-lighted streets, that I remembered I had been engaged to dine that very evening with the S- family. Though vexed with my forgetfulness (it would be rather awkward to explain) I couldn't help thinking that it had procured me a more amusing evening. And besides—business. The sacred business—.

In a barefooted negro who overtook me at a run and bolted down the landing-steps I recognized Jacobus's boatman, who must have been feeding in the kitchen. His usual "Good-night, sah!" as I went up my ship's ladder had a more cordial sound than on previous occasions.

Chapter 5

I KEPT MY word to Jacobus. I haunted his home. He was perpetually finding me there of an afternoon when he popped in for a moment from the "store." The sound of my voice talking to his Alice greeted him on his doorstep; and when he returned for good in the evening, ten to one he would hear it still going on in the veranda. I just nodded to him; he would sit down heavily and gently, and watch with a sort of approving anxiety my efforts to make his daughter smile.

I called her often "Alice," right before him; sometimes I would address her as "Miss Don't Care," and I exhausted myself in nonsensical chatter without succeeding once in taking her out of her peevish and tragic self. There were moments when I felt I must break out and start swearing at her till all was blue. And I fancied that had I done so Jacobus would not have moved a muscle. A sort of shady, intimate understanding seemed to have been established between us.

I must say the girl treated her father exactly in the same way she treated me.

And how could it have been otherwise? She treated me as she treated her father. She had never seen a visitor. She did not know how men behaved. I belonged to the low lot with whom her father did business at the port. I was of no account. So was her father. The only decent people in the world were the people of the island, who would have nothing to do with him because of something wicked he had done. This was apparently the explanation Miss Jacobus had given her of the household's isolated position. For she had to be told something! And I feel convinced that this version had been assented to by Jacobus. I must say the old woman was putting it forward with considerable gusto. It was on her lips the universal explanation, the universal allusion, the universal taunt.

One day Jacobus came in early and, beckoning me into the dining room, wiped his brow with a weary gesture and told me that he had managed to unearth a supply of quarter-bags.

"It's fourteen hundred your ship wanted, did you say, Captain?"

"Yes, yes!" I replied eagerly; but he remained calm. He looked more tired than I had ever seen him before.

"Well, Captain, you may go and tell your people that they can get that lot from my brother." As I remained open-mouthed at this, he added his usual placid formula of assurance:

"You'll find it correct, Captain."

"You spoke to your brother about it?" I was distinctly awed. "And for me? Because he must have known that my ship's the only one hung up for bags. How on earth—"

He wiped his brow again. I noticed that he was dressed with unusual care, in clothes in which I had never seen him before. He avoided my eye.

"You've heard people talk, of course. . . . That's true enough. He . . . I . . . We certainly. . . for several years . . ." His voice declined to a mere sleepy murmur. "You see I had something to tell him of, something which—"

His murmur stopped. He was not going to tell me what this something was. And I didn't care. Anxious to carry the news to my charterers, I ran back on the veranda to get my hat.

At the bustle I made the girl turned her eyes slowly in my direction, and even the old woman was checked in her knitting. I stopped a moment to exclaim excitedly:

"Your father's a brick, Miss Don't Care. That's what he is."

She beheld my elation in scornful surprise. Jacobus with unwonted familiarity seized my arm as I flew through the dining room, and breathed heavily at me a proposal about "A plate of soup" that evening. I answered distractedly: "Eh? What? Oh, thanks! Certainly. With pleasure," and tore myself away. Dine with him? Of course. The merest gratitude.

But some three hours afterwards, in the dusky, silent street, paved with cobble-stones, I became aware that it was not mere gratitude which was guiding my steps toward the house with the old garden, where for years no guest other than myself had ever dined. Mere gratitude does not gnaw at one's interior economy in that particular way. Hunger might; but I was not feeling particularly hungry for Jacobus's food.

On that occasion, too, the girl refused to come to the table.

My exasperation grew. The old woman cast malicious glances at me. I said suddenly to Jacobus: "Here! Put some chicken and salad on that plate." He obeyed without raising his eyes. I carried it with a knife and fork and a serviette out on the veranda. The garden was one mass of gloom, like a cemetery of flowers buried in the darkness, and she, in the chair, seemed to muse mournfully over the extinction of light and color. Only whiffs of heavy scent passed like wandering, fragrant souls of that departed multitude of blossoms. I talked volubly, jocularly, persuasively, tenderly; I talked in a subdued tone. To a listener it would have sounded like the murmur of a pleading lover. Whenever I paused expectantly there was only a deep silence. It was like offering food to a seated statue.

"I haven't been able to swallow a single morsel thinking of you out here starving yourself in the dark. It's positively cruel to be so obstinate. Think of my sufferings."

"Don't care."

I felt as if I could have done her some violence—shaken her, beaten her maybe. I said:

"Your absurd behavior will prevent me coming here any more."

"What's that to me?"

"You like it."

"It's false," she snarled.

My hand fell on her shoulder; and if she had flinched I verily believe I would have shaken her. But there was no movement and this immobility disarmed my anger.

"You do. Or you wouldn't be found on the veranda every day. Why are you here, then? There are plenty of rooms in the house. You have your own room to stay in—if you did not want to see me. But you do. You know you do."

I felt a slight shudder under my hand and released my grip as if frightened by that sign of animation in her body. The scented air of the garden came to us in a warm wave like a voluptuous and perfumed sigh.

"Go back to them," she whispered, almost pitifully.

As I re-entered the dining room I saw Jacobus cast down his eyes. I banged the plate on the table. At this demonstration of ill-humor he murmured something in an apologetic tone, and I turned on him viciously as if he were accountable to me for these "abominable eccentricities," I believe I called them.

"But I dare say Miss Jacobus here is responsible for most of this offensive manner," I added loftily.

She piped out at once in her brazen, ruffianly manner:

"Eh? Why don't you leave us in peace, my good fellow?"

I was astonished that she should dare before Jacobus. Yet what could he have done to repress her? He needed her too much. He raised a heavy, drowsy glance for an instant, then looked down again. She insisted with shrill finality:

"Haven't you done your business, you two? Well, then—"

She had the true Jacobus impudence, that old woman. Her mop of iron-gray hair was parted, on the side like a man's, raffishly, and she made as if to plunge her fork into it, as she used to do with the knitting-needle, but refrained. Her little black eyes sparkled venomously. I turned to my host at the head of the table—menacingly as it were.

"Well, and what do you say to that, Jacobus? Am I to take it that we have done with each other?"

I had to wait a little. The answer when it came was rather unexpected, and in quite another spirit than the question.

"I certainly think we might do some business yet with those potatoes of mine, Captain. You will find that—"

I cut him short.

"I've told you before that I don't trade."

His broad chest heaved without a sound in a noiseless sigh.

"Think it over, Captain," he murmured, tenacious and tranquil; and I burst into a jarring laugh, remembering how he had stuck to the circus-rider woman—the depth of passion under that placid surface, which even cuts with a riding-whip (so the legend had it) could never raffle into the semblance of a storm; something like the passion of a fish would be if one could imagine such a thing as a passionate fish.

That evening I experienced more distinctly than ever the sense of moral discomfort which always attended me in that house lying under the ban of all "decent" people. I refused to stay on and smoke after dinner; and when I put my hand into the thickly-cushioned palm of Jacobus, I said to myself that it would be for the last time under his roof. I pressed his bulky paw heartily nevertheless. Hadn't he got me out of a serious difficulty? To the few words of acknowledgment I was bound, and indeed quite willing, to utter, he answered by stretching his closed lips in his melancholy, glued-together smile.

"That will be all right, I hope, Captain," he breathed out weightily.

"What do you mean?" I asked, alarmed. "That your brother might yet—"

"Oh, no," he reassured me. "He . . . he's a man of his word, Captain."

My self-communion as I walked away from his door, trying to believe that this was for the last time, was not satisfactory. I was aware myself that I was not sincere in my reflections as to Jacobus's motives, and, of course, the very next day I went back again.

How weak, irrational, and absurd we are! How easily carried away whenever our awakened imagination brings us the irritating hint of a desire! I cared for the girl in a particular way, seduced by the moody expression of her face, by her obstinate silences, her rare, scornful words; by the perpetual pout of her closed lips, the black depths of her fixed gaze turned slowly upon me as if in contemptuous provocation, only to be averted next moment with an exasperating indifference.

Of course the news of my assiduity had spread all over the little town. I noticed a change in the manner of my acquaintances and even something different in the nods of the other captains, when meeting them at the landing-steps or in the offices where business called me. The old-maidish head clerk treated me with distant punctiliousness and, as it were, gathered his skirts round him for fear of contamination. It seemed to me that the very niggers on the quays turned to look after me as I passed; and as to Jacobus's boatman his "Good-night, sah!" when he put me on board was no longer merely cordial—it had a familiar, confidential sound as though we had been partners in some villainy.

My friend S- the elder passed me on the other side of the street with a wave of the hand and an ironic smile. The younger brother, the one they had married to an elderly shrew, he, on the strength of an older friendship and as if paying a debt of gratitude, took the liberty to utter a word of warning.

"You're doing yourself no good by your choice of friends, my dear chap," he said with infantile gravity.

As I knew that the meeting of the brothers Jacobus was the subject of excited comment in the whole of the sugary *Pearl of the Ocean* I wanted to know why I was blamed.

"I have been the occasion of a move which may end in a reconciliation surely desirable from the point of view of the proprieties—don't you know?"

"Of course, if that girl were disposed of it would certainly facilitate—" he mused sagely, then, inconsequential creature, gave me a light tap on the lower part of my waistcoat. "You old sinner," he cried jovially, "much you care for proprieties. But you had better look out for yourself, you know, with a personage like Jacobus who has no sort of reputation to lose."

He had recovered his gravity of a respectable citizen by that time and added regretfully:

"All the women of our family are perfectly scandalized."

But by that time I had given up visiting the S- family and the D- family. The elder ladies pulled such faces when I showed myself, and the multitude of related young ladies received me with such a variety of looks: wondering, awed, mocking (except Miss Mary, who spoke to me and looked at me with hushed, pained compassion as though I had been ill), that I had no difficulty in giving them all up. I would have given up the society of the whole town, for the sake of sitting near that girl, snarling and superb and barely clad in that flimsy, dingy, amber wrapper, open low at the throat. She looked, with the wild wisps of hair hanging down her tense face, as though she had just jumped out of bed in the panic of a fire.

She sat leaning on her elbow, looking at nothing. Why did she stay listening to my absurd chatter? And not only that; but why did she powder her face in preparation for my arrival? It seemed to be her idea of making a toilette, and in her untidy negligence a sign of great effort toward personal adornment.

But I might have been mistaken. The powdering might have been her daily practice and her presence in the veranda a sign of an indifference so complete as to take no account of my existence. Well, it was all one to me.

I loved to watch her slow changes of pose, to look at her long immobilities composed in the graceful lines of her body, to observe the mysterious narrow stare of her splendid black eyes, somewhat long in shape, half closed, contemplating the void. She was like a spellbound creature with the forehead of a goddess crowned by the disheveled magnificent hair of a gypsy tramp. Even her indifference was seductive. I felt myself growing attached to her by the bond of an irrealizable desire, for I kept my head—quite. And I put up with the moral discomfort of Jacobus's sleepy watchfulness, tranquil, and yet so expressive; as if there had been a tacit pact between us two. I put up with the insolence of the old woman's: "Aren't you ever going to leave us in peace, my good fellow?" with her taunts; with her brazen and sinister scolding. She was of the true Jacobus stock, and no mistake.

Directly I got away from the girl I called myself many hard names. What folly was this? I would ask myself. It was like being the slave of some depraved habit. And I returned to her with my head clear, my heart certainly free, not even moved by pity for that castaway (she was as much of a castaway as anyone ever wrecked on a desert island), but as if beguiled by some extraordinary promise. Nothing more unworthy could be imagined. The recollection of that tremulous whisper when I gripped her shoulder with one hand and held a plate of chicken with the other was enough to make me break all my good resolutions.

Her insulting taciturnity was enough sometimes to make one gnash one's teeth with rage. When she opened her mouth it was only to be abominably rude in harsh tones to the associate of her reprobate father; and the full approval of her aged relative was conveyed to her by offensive chuckles. If not that, then her remarks, always uttered in the tone of scathing contempt, were of the most appalling inanity.

How could it have been otherwise? That plump, ruffianly Jacobus old maid in the tight gray frock had never taught her any manners. Manners I suppose are not necessary for born castaways. No educational establishment could ever be induced to accept her as a pupil—on account of the proprieties, I imagine. And Jacobus had not been able to send her away anywhere. How could he have done it? Who with? Where to? He himself was not enough of an adventurer to think of settling down anywhere else. His passion had tossed him at the tail of a circus up and down strange coasts, but, the storm over, he had drifted back shamelessly where, social outcast as he was, he remained still a Jacobus—one of the oldest families on the island, older than the French even. There must have been a Jacobus in at the death of the last Dodo. . . . The girl had learned nothing, she had never listened to a general conversation, she knew nothing, she had heard of nothing. She could read certainly; but all the reading matter that ever came in her way were the newspapers provided for the captains' room of the "store." Jacobus had the habit of taking these sheets home now and then in a very stained and ragged condition.

As her mind could not grasp the meaning of any matters treated there except police-court reports and accounts of crimes, she had formed for herself a notion of the civilized world as a scene of murders, abductions, burglaries, stabbing affrays, and every sort of desperate violence. England and France, Paris and London (the only two towns of which she seemed to have heard), appeared to her sinks of abomination, reeking with blood, in contrast to her little island where petty larceny was about the standard of current misdeeds, with, now and then, some more pronounced crime—and that only among the imported coolie laborers on sugar estates or the negroes of the town. But in Europe these things were being done daily by a wicked population of white men among whom, as that ruffianly, aristocratic old Miss Jacobus pointed out, the wandering sailors, the associates of her precious papa, were the lowest of the low.

It was impossible to give her a sense of proportion. I suppose she figured England to herself as about the size of the *Pearl of the Ocean*; in which case it would certainly have been reeking with gore and a mere wreck of burgled houses from end to end. One could not make her understand that these horrors on which she fed her imagination were lost in the mass of orderly life like a few drops of blood in the ocean. She directed upon me for a moment the uncomprehending glance of her narrowed eyes and then would turn her scornful powdered face away without a word. She would not even take the trouble to shrug her shoulders.

At that time the batches of papers brought by the last mail reported a series of crimes in the East End of London, there was a sensational case of abduction in France and a fine display of armed robbery in Australia. One afternoon crossing the dining room I heard Miss Jacobus piping in the veranda with venomous animosity: "I don't know what your precious papa is plotting with that fellow. But he's just the sort of man who's capable of carrying you off far away somewhere and then cutting your throat some day for your money."

There was a good half of the length of the veranda between their chairs. I came out and sat down fiercely midway between them.

"Yes, that's what we do with girls in Europe," I began in a grimly matter-of-fact tone. I think Miss Jacobus was disconcerted by my sudden appearance. I turned upon her with cold ferocity:

"As to objectionable old women, they are first strangled quietly, then cut up into small pieces and thrown away, a bit here and a bit there. They vanish—"

I cannot go so far as to say I had terrified her. But she was troubled by my truculence, the more so because I had been always addressing her with a politeness she did not deserve. Her plump, knitting hands fell slowly on her knees. She said not a word while I fixed her with severe determination. Then as I turned away from her at last, she laid down her work gently and, with noiseless movements, retreated from the veranda. In fact, she vanished.

But I was not thinking of her. I was looking at the girl. It was what I was coming for daily; troubled, ashamed, eager; finding in my nearness to her a unique sensation which I indulged with dread, self-contempt, and deep pleasure, as if it were a secret vice bound to end in my undoing, like the habit of some drug or other which ruins and degrades its slave.

I looked her over, from the top of her disheveled head, down the lovely line of the shoulder, following the curve of the hip, the draped form of the long limb, right down to her fine ankle below a torn, soiled flounce; and as far as the point of the shabby, high-heeled, blue slipper, dangling from her well-shaped foot, which she moved slightly, with quick, nervous jerks, as if impatient of my presence. And in the scent of the massed flowers I seemed to breathe her special and inexplicable charm, the heady perfume of the everlastingly irritated captive of the garden.

I looked at her rounded chin, the Jacobus chin; at the full, red lips pouting in the powdered, sallow face; at the firm modelling of the cheek, the grains of white in the hairs of the straight somber eyebrows; at the long eyes, a narrowed gleam of liquid white and intense motionless black, with their gaze so empty of thought, and so absorbed in their fixity that she seemed to be staring at her own lonely image, in some far-off mirror hidden from my sight among the trees.

And suddenly, without looking at me, with the appearance of a person speaking to herself, she asked, in that voice slightly harsh yet mellow and always irritated:

"Why do you keep on coming here?"

"Why do I keep on coming here?" I repeated, taken by surprise. I could not have told her. I could not even tell myself with sincerity why I was coming there. "What's the good of you asking a question like that?"

"Nothing is any good," she observed scornfully to the empty air, her chin propped on her hand, that hand never extended to any man, that no one had ever grasped—for I had only grasped her shoulder once—that generous, fine, somewhat masculine hand. I knew well the peculiarly efficient shape—broad at the base, tapering at the fingers—of that hand, for which there was nothing in the world to lay hold of. I pretended to be playful.

"No! But do you really care to know?"

She shrugged indolently her magnificent shoulders, from which the dingy thin wrapper was slipping a little.

"Oh—never mind—never mind!"

There was something smoldering under those airs of lassitude. She exasperated me by the provocation of her nonchalance, by something elusive and defiant in her very form which I wanted to seize. I said roughly:

"Why? Don't you think I should tell you the truth?"

Her eyes glided my way for a sidelong look, and she murmured, moving only her full, pouting lips:

"I think you would not dare."

"Do you imagine I am afraid of you? What on earth. . . . Well, it's possible, after all, that I don't know exactly why I am coming here. Let us say, with Miss Jacobus, that it is for no good. You seem to believe the outrageous things she says, if you do have a row with her now and then."

She snapped out viciously:

"Who else am I to believe?"

"I don't know,"

I had to own, seeing her suddenly very helpless and condemned to moral solitude by the verdict of a respectable community. "You might believe me, if you chose."

She made a slight movement and asked me at once, with an effort as if making an experiment:

"What is the business between you and papa?"

"Don't you know the nature of your father's business? Come! He sells provisions to ships."

She became rigid again in her crouching pose.

"Not that. What brings you here—to this house?"

"And suppose it's you? You would not call that business? Would you? And now let us drop the subject. It's no use. My ship will be ready for sea the day after tomorrow."

She murmured a distinctly scared "So soon," and getting up quickly, went to the little table and poured herself a glass of water. She walked with rapid steps and with an indolent swaying of her whole young figure above the hips; when she passed near me I felt with tenfold force the charm of the peculiar, promising sensation I had formed the habit to seek near her. I thought with sudden dismay that this was the end of it; that after one more day I would be no longer able to come into this veranda, sit on this chair, and taste perversely the flavor of contempt in her indolent poses, drink in the provocation of her scornful looks, and listen to the curt, insolent remarks uttered in that harsh and seductive voice. As if my innermost nature had been altered by the action of some moral poison, I felt an abject dread of going to sea.

I had to exercise a sudden self-control, as one puts on a brake, to prevent myself jumping up to stride about, shout, gesticulate, make her a scene. What for? What about? I had no idea. It was just the relief of violence that I wanted; and I lolled back in my chair, trying to keep my lips formed in a smile; that half-indulgent, half-mocking smile which was my shield against the shafts of her contempt and the insulting sallies flung at me by the old woman.

She drank the water at a draught, with the avidity of raging thirst, and let herself fall on the nearest chair, as if utterly overcome. Her attitude, like certain tones of her voice, had in it something masculine: the knees apart in the ample wrapper, the clasped hands hanging between them, her body leaning forward, with drooping head. I stared at the heavy black coil of twisted hair. It was enormous, crowning the bowed head with a crushing and disdained glory. The escaped wisps hung straight down. And suddenly I perceived that the girl was trembling from head to foot, as though that glass of iced water had chilled her to the bone.

"What's the matter now?" I said, startled, but in no very sympathetic mood.

She shook her bowed, overweighted head and cried in a stifled voice but with a rising inflection:

"Go away! Go away! Go away!"

I got up then and approached her, with a strange sort of anxiety. I looked down at her round, strong neck, then stooped low enough to peep at her face. And I began to tremble a little myself.

"What on earth are you gone wild about, Miss Don't Care?"

She flung herself backwards violently, her head going over the back of the chair. And now it was her smooth, full, palpitating throat that lay exposed to my bewildered stare. Her eyes were nearly closed, with only a horrible white gleam under the lids as if she were dead.

"What has come to you?" I asked in awe. "What are you terrifying yourself with?"

She pulled herself together, her eyes open frightfully wide now. The tropical afternoon was lengthening the shadows on the hot, weary earth, the abode of obscure desires, of extravagant hopes, of unimaginable terrors.

"Never mind! Don't care!" Then, after a gasp, she spoke with such frightful rapidity that I could hardly make out the amazing words: "For if you were to shut me up in an empty place as smooth all round as the palm of my hand, I could always strangle myself with my hair."

For a moment, doubting my ears, I let this inconceivable declaration sink into me. It is ever impossible to guess at the wild thoughts that pass through the heads of our fellow-creatures. What monstrous imaginings of violence could have dwelt under the low forehead of that girl who had been taught to regard her father as "capable of anything" more in the light of a misfortune than that of a disgrace; as, evidently, something to be resented and feared rather than to be ashamed of? She seemed, indeed, as unaware of shame as of anything else in the world; but in her ignorance, her resentment and fear took a childish and violent shape.

Of course she spoke without knowing the value of words. What could she know of death—she who knew nothing of life? It was merely as the proof of her being beside herself with some odious apprehension, that this extraordinary speech had moved me, not to pity, but to a fascinated, horrified wonder. I had no idea what notion she had of her danger. Some sort of abduction. It was quite possible with the talk of that atrocious old woman. Perhaps she thought she could be carried off, bound hand and foot and even gagged. At that surmise I felt as if the door of a furnace had been opened in front of me.

"Upon my honor!" I cried. "You shall end by going crazy if you listen to that abominable old aunt of yours—"

I studied her haggard expression, her trembling lips. Her cheeks even seemed sunk a little. But how I, the associate of her disreputable father, the "lowest of the low" from the criminal Europe, could manage to reassure her I had no conception. She was exasperating.

"Heavens and earth! What do you think I can do?"

"I don't know."

Her chin certainly trembled. And she was looking at me with extreme attention. I made a step nearer to her chair.

"I shall do nothing. I promise you that. Will that do? Do you understand? I shall do nothing whatever, of any kind; and the day after tomorrow I shall be gone."

What else could I have said? She seemed to drink in my words with the thirsty avidity with which she had emptied the glass of water. She whispered tremulously, in that touching tone I had heard once before on her lips, and which thrilled me again with the same emotion:

"I would believe you. But what about papa—"

"He be hanged!" My emotion betrayed itself by the brutality of my tone. "I've had enough of your papa. Are you so stupid as to imagine that I am frightened of him? He can't make me do anything."

All that sounded feeble to me in the face of her ignorance. But I must conclude that the "accent of sincerity" has, as some people say, a really irresistible power. The effect was far beyond my hopes,—and even beyond my conception. To watch the change in the girl was like watching a miracle—the gradual but swift relaxation of her tense glance, of her stiffened muscles, of every fiber of her body. That black, fixed stare into which I had read a tragic meaning more than once, in which I had found a somber seduction, was perfectly empty now, void of all consciousness whatever, and not even aware any longer of my presence; it had become a little sleepy, in the Jacobus fashion.

But, man being a perverse animal, instead of rejoicing at my complete success, I beheld it with astounded and indignant eyes. There was something cynical in that unconcealed alteration, the true Jacobus shamelessness. I felt as though I had been cheated in some rather complicated deal into which I had entered against my better judgment. Yes, cheated without any regard for, at least, the forms of decency.

With an easy, indolent, and in its indolence supple, feline movement, she rose from the chair, so provokingly ignoring me now, that for very rage I held my ground within less than a foot of her. Leisurely and tranquil, behaving right before me with the ease of a person alone in a room, she extended her beautiful arms, with her hands clenched, her body swaying, her head thrown back a little, reveling contemptuously in a sense of relief, easing her limbs in freedom after all these days of crouching, motionless poses when she had been so furious and so afraid.

All this with supreme indifference, incredible, offensive, exasperating, like ingratitude doubled with treachery.

I ought to have been flattered, perhaps, but, on the contrary, my anger grew; her movement to pass by me as if I were a wooden post or a piece of furniture, that unconcerned movement brought it to a head.

I won't say I did not know what I was doing, but, certainly, cool reflection had nothing to do with the circumstance that next moment both my arms were round her waist. It was an impulsive action, as one snatches at something falling or escaping; and it had no hypocritical gentleness about it either. She had no time to make a sound, and the first kiss I planted on her closed lips was vicious enough to have been a bite.

She did not resist, and of course I did not stop at one. She let me go on, not as if she were inanimate—I felt her there, close against me, young, full of vigor, of life, a strong desirable creature, but as if she did not care in the least, in the absolute assurance of her safety, what I did or left undone. Our faces brought close together in this storm of haphazard caresses, her big, black, wide-open eyes looked into mine without the girl appearing either angry or pleased or moved in any way. In that steady gaze which seemed impersonally to watch my madness I could detect a slight surprise, perhaps—nothing more. I showered kisses upon her face and there did not seem to be any reason why this should not go on forever.

That thought flashed through my head, and I was on the point of desisting, when, all at once, she began to struggle with a sudden violence which all but freed her instantly, which revived my exasperation with her, indeed a fierce desire never to let her go any more. I tightened my embrace in time, gasping out: "No—you don't!" as if she were my mortal enemy. On her part not a word was said. Putting her hands against my chest, she pushed with all her might without succeeding to break the circle of my arms. Except that she seemed thoroughly awake now, her eyes gave me no clue whatever. To meet her black stare was like looking into a deep well, and I was totally unprepared for her change of tactics. Instead of trying to tear my hands apart, she flung herself upon my breast and with a downward, undulating, serpentine motion, a quick sliding dive, she got away from me smoothly. It was all very swift; I saw her pick up the tail of her wrapper and run for the door at the end of the veranda not very gracefully. She appeared to be limping a little—and then she vanished; the door swung behind her so noiselessly that I could not believe it was completely closed. I had a distinct suspicion of her black eye being at the crack to watch what I would do. I could not make up my mind whether to shake my fist in that direction or blow a kiss.

Chapter 6

EITHER WOULD HAVE been perfectly consistent with my feelings. I gazed at the door, hesitating, but in the end I did neither. The monition of some sixth sense—the sense of guilt, maybe, that sense which always acts too late, alas!—warned me to look round; and at once I became aware that the conclusion of this tumultuous episode was likely to be a matter of lively anxiety. Jacobus was standing in the doorway of the dining room. How long he had been there it was impossible to guess; and remembering my struggle with the girl I thought he must have been its mute witness from beginning to end. But this supposition seemed almost incredible. Perhaps that impenetrable girl had heard him come in and had got away in time.

He stepped on to the veranda in his usual manner, heavy-eyed, with glued lips. I marveled at the girl's resemblance to this man. Those long, Egyptian eyes, that low forehead of a stupid goddess, she had found in the sawdust of the circus; but all the rest of the face, the design and the modelling, the rounded chin, the very lips—all that was Jacobus, fined down, more finished, more expressive.

His thick hand fell on and grasped with force the back of a light chair (there were several standing about) and I perceived the chance of a broken head at the end of all this—most likely. My mortification was extreme. The scandal would be horrible; that was unavoidable. But how to act so as to satisfy myself I did not know. I stood on my guard and at any rate faced him. There was nothing else for it. Of one thing I was certain, that, however brazen my attitude, it could never equal the characteristic Jacobus impudence.

He gave me his melancholy, glued smile and sat down. I own I was relieved. The perspective of passing from kisses to blows had nothing particularly attractive in it. Perhaps—perhaps he had seen nothing? He behaved as usual, but he had never before found me alone on the veranda. If he had alluded to it, if he had asked: "Where's Alice?" or something of the sort, I would have been able to judge from the tone. He would give me no opportunity. The striking peculiarity was that he had never looked up at me yet. "He knows," I said to myself confidently. And my contempt for him relieved my disgust with myself.

"You are early home," I remarked.

"Things are very quiet; nothing doing at the store today," he explained with a cast-down air.

"Oh, well, you know, I am off," I said, feeling that this, perhaps, was the best thing to do.

"Yes," he breathed out. "Day after tomorrow."

This was not what I had meant; but as he gazed persistently on the floor, I followed the direction of his glance. In the absolute stillness of the house we stared at the high-heeled slipper the girl had lost in her flight. We stared. It lay overturned.

After what seemed a very long time to me, Jacobus hitched his chair forward, stooped with extended arm and picked it up. It looked a slender thing in his big, thick hands. It was not really a slipper, but a low shoe of blue, glazed kid, rubbed and shabby. It had straps to go over the instep, but the girl only thrust her feet in, after her slovenly manner. Jacobus raised his eyes from the shoe to look at me.

"Sit down, Captain," he said at last, in his subdued tone.

As if the sight of that shoe had renewed the spell, I gave up suddenly the idea of leaving the house there and then. It had become impossible. I sat down, keeping my eyes on the fascinating object. Jacobus turned his daughter's shoe over and over in his cushioned paws as if studying the way the thing was made. He contemplated the thin sole for a time; then glancing inside with an absorbed air:

"I am glad I found you here, Captain."

I answered this by some sort of grunt, watching him covertly. Then I added: "You won't have much more of me now."

He was still deep in the interior of that shoe on which my eyes too were resting.

"Have you thought any more of this deal in potatoes I spoke to you about the other day?"

"No, I haven't," I answered curtly. He checked my movement to rise by an austere, commanding gesture of the hand holding that fatal shoe. I remained seated and glared at him. "You know I don't trade."

"You ought to, Captain. You ought to."

I reflected. If I left that house now I would never see the girl again. And I felt I must see her once more, if only for an instant. It was a need, not to be reasoned with, not to be disregarded. No, I did not want to go away. I wanted to stay for one more experience of that strange provoking sensation and of indefinite desire, the habit of which had made me—me of all people!—dread the prospect of going to sea.

"Mr. Jacobus," I pronounced slowly. "Do you really think that upon the whole and taking various' matters into consideration—I mean everything, do you understand?—it would be a good thing for me to trade, let us say, with you?"

I waited for a while. He went on looking at the shoe which he held now crushed in the middle, the worn point of the toe and the high heel protruding on each side of his heavy fist.

"That will be all right," he said, facing me squarely at last.

"Are you sure?"

"You'll find it quite correct, Captain." He had uttered his habitual phrases in his usual placid, breath-saving voice and stood my hard, inquisitive stare sleepily without as much as a wink.

"Then let us trade," I said, turning my shoulder to him. "I see you are bent on it."

I did not want an open scandal, but I thought that outward decency may be bought too dearly at times. I included Jacobus, myself, the whole population of the island, in the same contemptuous disgust as though we had been partners in an ignoble transaction. And the remembered vision at sea, diaphanous and blue, of the *Pearl of the Ocean* at sixty miles off; the unsubstantial, clear marvel of it as if evoked by the art of a beautiful and pure magic, turned into a thing of horrors, too. Was this the fortune this vaporous and rare apparition had held for me in its hard heart, hidden within the shape as of fair dreams and mist? Was this my luck?

"I think"—Jacobus became suddenly audible after what seemed the silence of vile meditation—"that you might conveniently take some thirty tons. That would be about the lot, Captain."

"Would it? The lot! I dare say it would be convenient, but I haven't got enough money for that."

I had never seen him so animated.

"No!" he exclaimed with what I took for the accent of grim menace. "That's a pity." He paused, then, unrelenting: "How much money have you got, Captain?" he inquired with awful directness.

It was my turn to face him squarely. I did so and mentioned the amount I could dispose of. And I perceived that he was disappointed. He thought it over, his calculating gaze lost in mine, for quite a long time before he came out in a thoughtful tone with the rapacious suggestion:

"You could draw some more from your charterers. That would be quite easy, Captain."

"No, I couldn't," I retorted brusquely. "I've drawn my salary up to date, and besides, the ship's accounts are closed."

I was growing furious. I pursued: "And I'll tell you what: if I could do it I wouldn't." Then throwing off all restraint, I added: "You are a bit too much of a Jacobus, Mr. Jacobus."

The tone alone was insulting enough, but he remained tranquil, only a little puzzled, till something seemed to dawn upon him; but the unwonted light in his eyes died out instantly. As a Jacobus on his native heath, what a mere skipper chose to say could not touch him, outcast as he was. As a ship-chandler he could stand anything. All I caught of his mumble was a vague—"quite correct," than which nothing could have been more egregiously false at bottom—to my view, at least. But I remembered—I had never forgotten—that I must see the girl. I did not mean to go. I meant to stay in the house till I had seen her once more.

"Look here!" I said finally. "I'll tell you what I'll do. I'll take as many of your confounded potatoes as my money will buy, on condition that you go off at once down to the wharf to see them loaded in the lighter and sent alongside the ship straight away. Take the invoice and a signed receipt with you. Here's the key of my desk. Give it to Burns. He will pay you.

He got up from his chair before I had finished speaking, but he refused to take the key. Burns would never do it. He wouldn't like to ask him even.

"Well, then," I said, eyeing him slightingly, "there's nothing for it, Mr. Jacobus, but you must wait on board till I come off to settle with you."

"That will be all right, Captain. I will go at once."

He seemed at a loss what to do with the girl's shoe he was still holding in his fist. Finally, looking dully at me, he put it down on the chair from which he had risen.

"And you, Captain? Won't you come along, too, just to see—"

"Don't bother about me. I'll take care of myself."

He remained perplexed for a moment, as if trying to understand; and then his weighty: "Certainly, certainly, Captain," seemed to be the outcome of some sudden thought. His big chest heaved. Was it a sigh? As he went out to hurry off those potatoes he never looked back at me.

I waited till the noise of his footsteps had died out of the dining room, and I waited a little longer. Then turning toward the distant door I raised my voice along the veranda:

"Alice!"

Nothing answered me, not even a stir behind the door. Jacobus's house might have been made empty for me to make myself at home in. I did not call again. I had become aware of a great discouragement. I was mentally jaded, morally dejected. I turned to the garden again, sitting down with my elbows spread on the low balustrade, and took my head in my hands.

The evening closed upon me. The shadows lengthened, deepened, mingled together into a pool of twilight in which the flower-beds glowed like colored embers; whiffs of heavy scent came to me as if the dusk of this hemisphere were but the dimness of a temple and the garden an enormous censer swinging before the altar of the stars. The colors of the blossoms deepened, losing their glow one by one.

The girl, when I turned my head at a slight noise, appeared to me very tall and slender, advancing with a swaying limp, a floating and uneven motion which ended in the sinking of her shadowy form into the deep low chair. And I don't know why or whence I received the impression that she had come too late. She ought to have appeared at my call. She ought to have . . . It was as if a supreme opportunity had been missed.

I rose and took a seat close to her, nearly opposite her armchair. Her ever discontented voice addressed me at once, contemptuously:

"You are still here."

I pitched mine low.

"You have come out at last."

"I came to look for my shoe—before they bring in the lights."

It was her harsh, enticing whisper, subdued, not very steady, but its low tremulousness gave me no thrill now. I could only make out the oval of her face, her uncovered throat, the long, white gleam of her eyes. She was mysterious enough. Her hands were resting on the arms of the chair. But where was the mysterious and provoking sensation which was like the perfume of her flower-like youth? I said quietly:

"I have got your shoe here." She made no sound and I continued: "You had better give me your foot and I will put it on for you."

She made no movement. I bent low down and groped for her foot under the flounces of the wrapper. She did not withdraw it and I put on the shoe, buttoning the instep-strap. It was an inanimate foot. I lowered it gently to the floor.

"If you buttoned the strap you would not be losing your shoe, Miss Don't Care," I said, trying to be playful without conviction. I felt more like wailing over the lost illusion of vague desire, over the sudden conviction that I would never find again near her the strange, half-evil, half-tender sensation which had given its acrid flavor to so many days, which had made her appear tragic and promising, pitiful and provoking. That was all over.

"Your father picked it up," I said, thinking she may just as well be told of the fact.

"I am not afraid of papa—by himself," she declared scornfully.

"Oh! It's only in conjunction with his disreputable associates, strangers, the 'riff-raff of Europe' as your charming aunt or great-aunt says—men like me, for instance—that you—"

"I am not afraid of you," she snapped out.

"That's because you don't know that I am now doing business with your father. Yes, I am in fact doing exactly what he wants me to do. I've broken my promise to you. That's the sort of man I am. And now—aren't you afraid? If you believe what that dear, kind, truthful old lady says you ought to be."

It was with unexpected modulated softness that the affirmed:

"No. I am not afraid." She hesitated. . . . "Not now."

"Quite right. You needn't be. I shall not see you again before I go to sea." I rose and stood near her chair. "But I shall often think of you in this old garden, passing under the trees over there, walking between these gorgeous flower-beds. You must love this garden—"

"I love nothing."

I heard in her sullen tone the faint echo of that resentfully tragic note which I had found once so provoking. But it left me unmoved except for a sudden and weary conviction of the emptiness of all things under Heaven.

"Good-bye, Alice," I said.

She did not answer, she did not move. To merely take her hand, shake it, and go away seemed impossible, almost improper. I stooped without haste and pressed my lips to her smooth forehead. This was the moment when I realized clearly with a sort of terror my complete detachment from that unfortunate creature. And as I lingered in that cruel self-knowledge I felt the light touch of her arms falling languidly on my neck and received a hasty, awkward, haphazard kiss which missed my lips. No! She was not afraid; but I was no longer moved. Her arms slipped off my neck slowly, she made no sound, the deep wicker armchair creaked slightly; only a sense of my dignity prevented me fleeing headlong from that catastrophic revelation.

I traversed the dining room slowly. I thought: She's listening to my footsteps; she can't help it; she'll hear me open and shut that door. And I closed it as gently behind me as if I had been a thief retreating with his ill-gotten booty. During that stealthy act I experienced the last touch of emotion in that house, at the thought of the girl I had left sitting there in the obscurity, with her heavy hair and empty eyes as black as the night itself, staring into the walled garden, silent, warm, odorous with the perfume of imprisoned flowers, which, like herself, were lost to sight in a world buried in darkness.

The narrow, ill-lighted, rustic streets I knew so well on my way to the harbor were extremely quiet. I felt in my heart that the further one ventures the better one understands how everything in our life is common, short, and empty; that it is in seeking the unknown in our sensations that we discover how mediocre are our attempts and how soon defeated! Jacobus's boatman was waiting at the steps with an unusual air of readiness. He put me alongside the ship, but did not give me his confidential "Good-evening, sah," and, instead of shoving off at once, remained holding by the ladder.

I was a thousand miles from commercial affairs, when on the dark quarter-deck Mr. Burns positively rushed at me, stammering with excitement. He had been pacing the deck distractedly for hours awaiting my arrival. Just before sunset a lighter loaded with potatoes had come alongside with that fat ship-chandler himself sitting on the pile of sacks. He was now stuck immovable in the cabin. What was the meaning of it all? Surely I did not—

"Yes, Mr. Burns, I did," I cut him short. He was beginning to make gestures of despair when I stopped that, too, by giving him the key of my desk and desiring him, in a tone which admitted of no argument, to go below at once, pay Mr. Jacobus's bill, and send him out of the ship.

"I don't want to see him," I confessed frankly, climbing the poop-ladder. I felt extremely tired. Dropping on the seat of the skylight, I gave myself up to idle gazing at the lights about the quay and at the black mass of the mountain on the south side of the harbor. I never heard Jacobus leave the ship with every single sovereign of my ready cash in his pocket. I never heard anything till, a long time afterwards, Mr. Burns, unable to contain himself any longer, intruded upon me with his ridiculously angry lamentations at my weakness and good nature.

"Of course, there's plenty of room in the after-hatch. But they are sure to go rotten down there. Well! I never heard . . . seventeen tons! I suppose I must hoist in that lot first thing tomorrow morning."

"I suppose you must. Unless you drop them overboard. But I'm afraid you can't do that. I wouldn't mind myself, but it's forbidden to throw rubbish into the harbor, you know."

"That is the truest word you have said for many a day, sir—rubbish. That's just what I expect they are. Nearly eighty good gold sovereigns gone; a perfectly clean sweep of your drawer, sir. Bless me if I understand!"

As it was impossible to throw the right light on this commercial transaction I left him to his lamentations and under the impression that I was a hopeless fool. Next day I did not go ashore. For one thing, I had no money to go ashore with—no, not enough to buy a cigarette. Jacobus had made a clean sweep. But that was not the only reason. The *Pearl of the Ocean* had in a few short hours grown odious to me. And I did not want to meet anyone. My reputation had suffered. I knew I was the object of unkind and sarcastic comments.

The following morning at sunrise, just as our stern-fasts had been let go and the tug plucked us out from between the buoys, I saw Jacobus standing up in his boat. The nigger was pulling hard; several baskets of provisions for ships were stowed between the thwarts. The father of Alice was going his morning round. His countenance was tranquil and friendly. He raised his arm and shouted something with great heartiness. But his voice was of the sort that doesn't carry any distance; all I could catch faintly, or rather guess at, were the words "next time" and "quite correct." And it was only of these last that I was certain. Raising my arm perfunctorily for all response, I turned away. I rather resented the familiarity of the thing. Hadn't I settled accounts finally with him by means of that potato bargain?

This being a harbor story it is not my purpose to speak of our passage. I was glad enough to be at sea, but not with the gladness of old days. Formerly I had no memories to take away with me. I shared in the blessed forgetfulness of sailors, that forgetfulness natural and invincible, which resembles innocence in so far that it prevents self-examination. Now however I remembered the girl. During the first few days I was forever questioning myself as to the nature of facts and sensations connected with her person and with my conduct.

And I must say also that Mr. Burns' intolerable fussing with those potatoes was not calculated to make me forget the part which I had played. He looked upon it as a purely commercial transaction of a particularly foolish kind, and his devotion—if it was devotion and not mere cussedness as I came to regard it before long—inspired him with a zeal to minimize my loss as much as possible. Oh, yes! He took care of those infamous potatoes with a vengeance, as the saying goes.

Everlastingly, there was a tackle over the after-hatch and everlastingly the watch on deck were pulling up, spreading out, picking over, rebagging, and lowering down again, some part of that lot of potatoes. My bargain with all its remotest associations, mental and visual—the garden of flowers and scents, the girl with her provoking contempt and her tragic loneliness of a hopeless castaway—was everlastingly dangled before my eyes, for thousands of miles along the open sea. And as if by a satanic refinement of irony it was accompanied by a most awful smell. Whiffs from decaying potatoes pursued me on the poop, they mingled with my thoughts, with my food, poisoned my very dreams. They made an atmosphere of corruption for the ship.

I remonstrated with Mr. Burns about this excessive care. I would have been well content to batten the hatch down and let them perish under the deck.

That perhaps would have been unsafe. The horrid emanations might have flavored the cargo of sugar. They seemed strong enough to taint the very ironwork. In addition Mr. Burns made it a personal matter. He assured me he knew how to treat a cargo of potatoes at sea—had been in the trade as a boy, he said. He meant to make my loss as small as possible. What between his devotion—it must have been devotion—and his vanity, I positively dared not give him the order to throw my commercial-venture overboard. I believe he would have refused point blank to obey my lawful command. An unprecedented and comical situation would have been created with which I did not feel equal to deal.

I welcomed the coming of bad weather as no sailor had ever done. When at last I hove the ship to, to pick up the pilot outside Port Philip Heads, the after-hatch had not been opened for more than a week and I might have believed that no such thing as a potato had ever been on board.

It was an abominable day, raw, blustering, with great squalls of wind and rain; the pilot, a cheery person, looked after the ship and chatted to me, streaming from head to foot; and the heavier the lash of the downpour the more pleased with himself and everything around him he seemed to be. He rubbed his wet hands with a satisfaction, which to me, who had stood that kind of thing for several days and nights, seemed inconceivable in any non-aquatic creature.

"You seem to enjoy getting wet, Pilot," I remarked.

He had a bit of land round his house in the suburbs and it was of his garden he was thinking. At the sound of the word garden, unheard, unspoken for so many days, I had a vision of gorgeous color, of sweet scents, of a girlish figure crouching in a chair. Yes. That was a distinct emotion breaking into the peace I had found in the sleepless anxieties of my responsibility during a week of dangerous bad weather. The Colony, the pilot explained, had suffered from unparalleled drought. This was the first decent drop of water they had had for seven months. The root crops were lost. And, trying to be casual, but with visible interest, he asked me if I had perchance any potatoes to spare.

Potatoes! I had managed to forget them. In a moment I felt plunged into corruption up to my neck. Mr. Burns was making eyes at me behind the pilot's back.

Finally, he obtained a ton, and paid ten pounds for it. This was twice the price of my bargain with Jacobus. The spirit of covetousness woke up in me. That night, in harbor, before I slept, the Custom House galley came alongside. While his underlings were putting seals on the storerooms, the officer in charge took me aside confidentially. "I say, Captain, you don't happen to have any potatoes to sell."

Clearly there was a potato famine in the land. I let him have a ton for twelve pounds and he went away joyfully. That night I dreamt of a pile of gold in the form of a grave in which a girl was buried, and woke up callous with greed. On calling at my ship-broker's office, that man, after the usual business had been transacted, pushed his spectacles up on his forehead.

"I was thinking, Captain, that coming from the *Pearl of the Ocean* you may have some potatoes to sell."

I said negligently: "Oh, yes, I could spare you a ton. Fifteen pounds."

He exclaimed: "I say!" But after studying my face for a while accepted my terms with a faint grimace. It seems that these people could not exist without potatoes. I could. I didn't want to see a potato as long as I lived; but the demon of lucre had taken possession of me. How the news got about I don't know, but, returning on board rather late, I found a small group of men of the coster type hanging about the waist, while Mr. Burns walked to and fro the quarterdeck loftily, keeping a triumphant eye on them. They had come to buy potatoes.

"These chaps have been waiting here in the sun for hours," Burns whispered to me excitedly. "They have drank the water-cask dry. Don't you throw away your chances, sir. You are too good-natured."

I selected a man with thick legs and a man with a cast in his eye to negotiate with; simply because they were easily distinguishable from the rest. "You have the money on you?" I inquired, before taking them down into the cabin.

"Yes, sir," they answered in one voice, slapping their pockets. I liked their air of quiet determination. Long before the end of the day all the potatoes were sold at about three times the price I had paid for them.

Mr. Burns, feverish and exulting, congratulated himself on his skillful care of my commercial venture, but hinted plainly that I ought to have made more of it.

That night I did not sleep very well. I thought of Jacobus by fits and starts, between snatches of dreams concerned with castaways starving on a desert island covered with flowers. It was extremely unpleasant. In the morning, tired and unrefreshed, I sat down and wrote a long letter to my owners, giving them a carefully-thought-out scheme for the ship's employment in the East and about the China Seas for the next two years. I spent the day at that task and felt somewhat more at peace when it was done.

Their reply came in due course. They were greatly struck with my project; but considering that, notwithstanding the unfortunate difficulty with the bags (which they trusted I would know how to guard against in the future), the voyage showed a very fair profit, they thought it would be better to keep the ship in the sugar trade—at least for the present.

I turned over the page and read on:

"We have had a letter from our good friend Mr. Jacobus. We are pleased to see how well you have hit it off with him; for, not to speak of his assistance in the unfortunate matter of the bags, he writes us that should you, by using all possible dispatch, manage to bring the ship back early in the season he would be able to give us a good rate of freight. We have no doubt that your best endeavors . . . etcetera, etcetera."

I dropped the letter and sat motionless for a long time. Then I wrote my answer (it was a short one) and went ashore myself to post it. But I passed one letter-box, then another, and in the end found myself going up Collins Street with the letter still in my pocket—against my heart. Collins Street at four o'clock in the afternoon is not exactly a desert solitude; but I had never felt more isolated from the rest of mankind as when I walked that day its crowded pavement, battling desperately with my thoughts and feeling already vanquished.

There came a moment when the awful tenacity of Jacobus, the man of one passion and of one idea, appeared to me almost heroic. He had not given me up. He had gone again to his odious brother. And then he appeared to me odious himself. Was it for his own sake or for the sake of the poor girl? And on that last supposition the memory of the kiss which missed my lips appalled me; for whatever he had seen, or guessed at, or risked, he knew nothing of that. Unless the girl had told him. How could I go back to fan that fatal spark with my cold breath? No, no, that unexpected kiss had to be paid for at its full price.

At the first letter-box I came to I stopped and reaching into my breast-pocket I took out the letter—it was as if I were plucking out my very heart—and dropped it through the slit. Then I went straight on board.

I wondered what dreams I would have that night; but as it turned out I did not sleep at all. At breakfast I informed Mr. Burns that I had resigned my command.

He dropped his knife and fork and looked at me with indignation.

"You have, sir! I thought you loved the ship."

"So I do, Burns," I said. "But the fact is that the Indian Ocean and everything that is in it has lost its charm for me. I am going home as passenger by the Suez Canal."

"Everything that is in it," he repeated angrily. "I've never heard anybody talk like this. And to tell you the truth, sir, all the time we have been together I've never quite made you out. What's one ocean more than another? Charm, indeed!"

He was really devoted to me, I believe. But he cheered up when I told him that I had recommended him for my successor.

"Anyhow," he remarked, "let people say what they like, this Jacobus has served your turn. I must admit that this potato business has paid extremely well. Of course, if only you had—"

"Yes, Mr. Burns," I interrupted. "Quite a smile of fortune."

But I could not tell him that it was driving me out of the ship I had learned to love. And as I sat heavy-hearted at that parting, seeing all my plans destroyed, my modest future endangered—for this command was like a foot in the stirrup for a young man—he gave up completely for the first time his critical attitude.

"A wonderful piece of luck!" he said.